Return to Black Rock

After serving fifteen years for his father's murder, a crime he didn't commit, Glenn Price is looking forward to his first day of freedom. But his enjoyment is short-lived when bounty hunter Randall Nash captures him the moment he steps out of jail.

Randall drags Glenn back to Black Rock, whose townsfolk nearly lynched him before. Within minutes of returning, Glenn faces the mob again when the corrupt sheriff charges him with another unjustified allegation of murder.

Can Glenn clear his name and find the real killer before the townsfolk invite him to a necktie party?

Return to Black Rock

Scott Connor

A Black Horse Western

ROBERT HALE · LONDON

Ⓢ Scott Connor 2006
First published in Great Britain 2006

ISBN-10: 0-7090-8170-7
ISBN-13: 978-0-7090-8170-8

Robert Hale Limited
Clerkenwell House
Clerkenwell Green
London EC1R 0HT

Typeset by
Derek Doyle & Associates, Shaw Heath
Printed and bound in Great Britain by
Antony Rowe Limited, Wiltshire

CHAPTER 1

The deep red rays of the rising sun stabbed into Glenn Price's eyes and the early morning chill wrapped him in its icy embrace. But as he enjoyed his first taste of freedom for fifteen years, he welcomed the brightness with his eyes wide open and drew the cold air deep into his chest.

Despite the cuffs that clamped his hands and the chain that linked his wrists to the metal collar around his neck, Glenn smiled as he looked at the sky, enjoying seeing clouds without the frame of his barred cell window.

Behind him, the heavy double doors of Leavenworth State penitentiary clattered shut, but Glenn still hadn't obtained the solitude he craved. Two guards had followed him out to remove his chains.

One guard shoved Glenn forward, but the heavy metal ball he dragged along behind him stopped him from stumbling more than a pace. Then he shuffled round on the spot and held out his clamped hands to the guards. These men stared at him, arrogant gleams lighting their eyes as they prolonged the moment before they had to give him his freedom.

'Come on,' Glenn snapped. 'Release me.'

'Be quiet,' one guard muttered. 'You go when we say so, not you.'

Glenn bit his bottom lip, accepting that they were looking for another excuse to delay his release. He was already a week late in leaving, but now that he was on the outside, they had no good reason for delaying again.

The guards exchanged a glance and a sly wink, then one drew a key from his pocket. Instead of setting it to Glenn's locks, he dangled it between outstretched fingers, tantalizingly close to Glenn's nose. Then he threw it to the other guard, who circled around Glenn.

They hurled taunts at him, but they had no impact on a man who was now free and knew the indignities they could inflict on him had to end soon.

Sure enough, with Glenn not rising to their baiting the guards' taunts petered out and the taller man signified that he should face him. Glenn moved, but the other guard paced behind him then slammed both fists down on his shoulders, knocking him to his knees. In a co-ordinated move, the other guard kicked out. His boot crunched into Glenn's chin and sent him reeling.

Then the blows and kicks came fast and hard as the guards availed themselves of their last opportunity to beat their prisoner.

At first Glenn fought back, even returning a glancing blow with a bunched coil of chains across one of the guards' chest, but that only fuelled them on to batter him with even more grim determination.

6

Glenn rolled away from their flailing limbs, gaining his freedom, and saw that a man was walking down the trail towards them. This man was leading two horses. He was rangy and Glenn was sure he recognized him, but the memory wouldn't form. Then the guards surrounded him again and he could do nothing but curl into a ball.

He lay with his eyes clamped shut, but the blows didn't restart.

Glenn heard the newcomer's steady footfalls closing on him and he guessed this man's arrival had saved him from a lengthier beating. Inside, the guards were used to there being no witnesses to their actions, but now they were outside the prison walls, perhaps they didn't want to risk being seen. And in confirmation of Glenn's belief, they rolled him over, jabbed the key into the locks, then dragged the chains from his wrists, ankles and neck.

Then they hurried away and slammed the prison doors shut behind them.

Glenn cracked open an eye and saw one guard peering out of the small inset door at him, then at the man. Then that door rattled shut and Glenn could at last enjoy his freedom.

He lay back, flexing his muscles and finding that his resilience, which had pulled him through fifteen years of hell, had again saved him from suffering too much damage from his final beating.

Then he remembered the approaching man and swung his head to the side. He watched the man stomp to a halt and peer down at him from under a lowered hat, the early-morning sun that silhouetted

7

his form masking his features.

Again, that flash of an old memory battered at Glenn's thoughts.

He narrowed his eyes, slowly resolving the man's features and, in a pained moment, that memory exploded across his mind as he recognized the man as being Randall Nash, but by then Randall was lunging down and grabbing his collar.

'Glenn Milton Price,' Randall said, then hoisted him up to peer into his eyes. 'Welcome to the outside world. Your suffering is about to start.'

'You got no reason to hold me,' Glenn shouted, shaking the ropes that tied his hands. 'I'm a free man now and I got rights.'

Randall pushed Glenn to the ground. 'Yeah, yeah, and maybe soon I'll let you enjoy those rights.'

Glenn snorted his breath through his nostrils then grabbed the bowl of broth from beside the fire.

His first day of freedom had not lived up to his expectations. Randall Nash, the bounty hunter who had captured him fifteen years ago, was the man who had accosted him outside the prison.

Randall had then tied him up, ignoring his complaints, slung him over a horse and ridden him off down the trail. Only now, with sundown approaching, had he halted his relentless journey west and let him sit and eat, but he still hadn't removed his bonds.

'What you want with me this time?' Glenn watched Randall through the flickering firelight. When Nash didn't respond, Glenn wolfed down his meal in five

8

ravenous gulps, then threw his tin bowl to the ground where it rattled to a halt. 'Damn it, Randall. You got to tell me why you've captured me.'

From under a lowered hat, Randall considered the bowl then looked up at Glenn, his craggy features as resolute as Glenn had remembered them.

'You've been a prisoner. You know how it works. You earn your rights. You spent the day roped up and with your head down, but if you don't try to escape tonight, I'll let you ride upright tomorrow. If you try anything, you won't.'

'I might not try to escape if you tell me why you seized me the moment I came out of jail. I ain't exactly had much opportunity to commit no crimes recently.'

Randall collected the bowl and placed it beside his own.

'Then I'll tell you. You got a two-hundred-and-fifty-dollar bounty on your head. It ain't much, but I intend to collect.'

'For what crime?'

Randall stoked the fire with a branch then hurled it into the flames.

'Last week, Myron Cole was murdered.'

Glenn blinked, hard. 'But I was in prison. I got the best alibi a man could want to prove I didn't kill him.'

'You have, but even men like you have friends, and you can sure hire men to kill the people you hate.'

'Not me.' Glenn shook a fist at Randall. 'And nobody can prove I did.'

'Proof ain't my problem. I just bring 'em in for the

bounty.' Randall raised his eyebrows as he leaned forward. 'But you know the way I work. If I get a better offer, I might let you go. And I reckon the name of the man who killed Myron Cole will be worth more than your hide.'

'But I don't know nothing about who killed him.'

'Then consider the man who's investigating his murder and the man who I'll be handing you over to.' Randall leaned back. 'Sheriff Emerson Price of Black Rock, your cousin and the nephew of the man you killed.'

Glenn couldn't help but gulp. 'I ain't going back to Black Rock. The whole town tried to lynch me last time.'

'They did.' Randall produced a wide smile. 'So you got three days to start talking, or this time they might finish what they started.'

CHAPTER 2

For the last fifteen years Glenn had obeyed the prisoner's rules of survival. Now that he was on the outside, he found they were no different from what they had been on the inside.

He had to appear to be docile and that he was pleasing his captor so that he could earn the privileges that might give him an opportunity to escape.

But one thing hadn't changed in Randall Nash in the fifteen years since Glenn had last encountered him – his attentiveness. Randall never relaxed his guard, even when apparently asleep, so although Glenn got to ride upright, he knew that running would gain him no more than a few minutes of freedom.

His conversation with Randall on the first evening after his release had convinced him that he knew Randall's plan, and he resolved to not let it affect him. But after suffering two days of brooding travel towards Black Rock, and with Randall setting off before first light on the third day to ensure he reached his destination by sundown, Glenn became increasingly agitated.

Late in the morning, he had at last to voice his concern.

'It won't work, Randall,' he grunted as he peered sideways at his captor.

Randall rode on for a while before slowly he turned in the saddle to consider Glenn.

'What won't?'

'Your attempt to get me to talk. You don't plan to take me to Black Rock. You hope the nearer I get to town, the more I'll panic and the more likely it is I'll tell you who killed Myron Cole.' Glenn stared at Randall, but received a firm stare back.

'You're right and you're wrong. I *do* reckon you'll talk before we reach Black Rock.' Randall's smile was grim. 'But even if you don't, I'm still handing you over to Sheriff Price.'

Glenn lowered his voice, trying to inject as much assurance into his tone as he could manage.

'But no matter how tough you act, I reckon you're a fair man, so think about this . . . taking me in to *that* town and *that* man will get me killed whether I had anything to do with Myron's murder or not.'

'I know your opinion of the Price family. After all, you did kill one of 'em. And you are one of 'em.'

'I didn't kill nobody. And John Price was my adoptive father. I'm not a real Price.'

Randall snorted a chuckle. 'So now that you're in the mood to talk, is there anything else you want to tell me?'

'Except for the fact that I didn't kill John Price and I don't know nothing about Myron Cole's murder, no.'

'So you've said, and maybe when Sheriff Price has you in a cell, I might believe you. But that ain't my concern. I just bring 'em in for the bounty.'

Randall stared at him with his lips pursed. Glenn reckoned he was aiming for his silence and his firm gaze to force him to continue talking and perhaps inadvertently reveal something.

But Glenn swung round to face ahead, vowing to stay quiet all the way to Black Rock if necessary. Unfortunately, that wouldn't be for long. They were approaching a meandering creek that would eventually swing past the towering rock that gave the town its name. Glenn judged that they had four hours of steady riding before they reached town. And so he had slightly more than four hours to live.

Fifteen years had passed since he had last seen Black Rock, and fifteen years and a month since that fateful day when his father had sent him to see Matlock Langhorne to try to sell him a cabinet. And as he had done many times over those fifteen years, he couldn't help but let his mind drift back to that day. . . .

It had been a fine summer day filled with the promise that every day in a booming town brought. And as Glenn had just turned eighteen and had his whole life stretching ahead, full of possibilities, that promise was even stronger. Glenn was sure he would achieve plenty with his life. He was confident in his abilities and although his father had provided him with few chances to demonstrate those abilities, obtaining a good return for the cabinet was an excellent opportunity to show him what he could do.

'I'll give you twenty dollars,' Matlock Langhorne, Mayor Adam Price's assistant, had said, standing in the doorway to the mayor's office on the outskirts of Black Rock.

Glenn rubbed his chin, feigning that he was thinking about his offer. His father had told him to accept fifteen, but Glenn reckoned this was a chance for him to make his pa proud of him and come away with even more.

'Twenty sounds good, but thirty sounds even better.' Glenn smiled. 'And forty will get you the cabinet this very afternoon.'

'It is not worth thirty.'

'Myron Cole reckons it might be. He's already offered me twenty-five.'

Matlock narrowed his eyes as he peered at Glenn, trying to discern whether this was true. In reality, Myron had offered Glenn a kick up the butt if he tried to sell him that cabinet again, but Glenn returned his gaze.

'Maybe I will go to thirty,' Matlock said, 'but not a cent more.'

Glenn bit his tongue, avoiding shouting out his pleasure.

'I'll have to agree that with Myron. But if he offers thirty-five, I will sell to him.' Glenn raised his eyebrows. 'Unless you're prepared to go to forty.'

'I am not,' Matlock snapped, then softened his expression as he patted Glenn's shoulder. 'But you're doing fine with this negotiating. You're already better at it than John ever was.'

Despite his determination to appear a shrewd

businessman, Glenn beamed with pleasure.

'I'm doing my best.'

'That mean John is trusting you with more respon-sibility?'

'A bit. I ain't so good with my hands as he is.' Glenn suppressed a wince as the memory came to him of the collapsing table, his first attempt to make a piece of furniture on his own. 'But I reckon I can take care of the customer side of the business.'

'And you're doing fine.'

With Matlock being so friendly, Glenn couldn't help but be honest.

'Actually, Pa only sent me because he couldn't come. He had an errand out of town. But if I can get a good price, he might let me carry on with the sell-ing.'

Glenn gulped, wondering if that weak admission might make Matlock lower his offer, but Matlock had a glazed look as he peered over Glenn's shoulder and down the road. Glenn judged that he hadn't heard his last comment.

'He's not in . . .' Matlock shook himself. 'Well, I have an errand to run, too. So you have fifteen minutes to check with Myron and then my offer is closed.'

Glenn nodded and headed off. Myron's smithy was a quarter-mile out of town and he always noticed anyone who approached. So he considered slipping in to Bill Cooke's mercantile to tell his sister the good news, but a sideways glance confirmed that Matlock was still looking at him. And that meant he'd have to risk going to the smithy and receiving that kicking.

Ten minutes later, he sat on the ground outside the smithy nursing several bruises while trying to appear nonchalant and unconcerned at being thrown outside. But at least he'd confirmed that Myron's tough stance hadn't been a bargaining tool and he really didn't want to buy the cabinet.

Hobbling slightly, he hurried into town and to the mayor's office, but Matlock still hadn't returned from his errand. He waited another fifteen minutes, but gradually a worry that he hadn't closed the deal on thirty dollars after all replaced his elation. So he mooched around town, looking for Matlock. When he failed to locate him he dawdled back to their house.

Glenn lived with his father and sister a mile out of town on the other side of a hill and out of view of the town. Glenn usually took the shortest route home, but with the unclosed deal preying on his mind, he wandered around the hill, keeping the town, and so the possibility of seeing Matlock return, in view for as long as possible.

But the town remained as silent and as untroubled as it usually did.

He was just resolving to return to town in an hour when he noticed his father's bay standing in the small corral at the side of the house. His father had said he'd be gone for the most of the day, so this surprised Glenn and, for a reason he couldn't identify, worried him. A tremor in his guts put him on guard and he approached the house while still looking around.

His heart hammered with an insistent patter. The

16

creaking then the banging of the door as it swung open and closed rattled his nerves even further. So by the time he stood in the doorway, he was sweating heavily and had to wipe the moisture from his brow to stop it burning his eyes. And in the darkened interior, for a moment, his dazzled eyesight couldn't discern what he was seeing.

Then he realized.

His father was lying beside the very same cabinet that he'd so nearly sold to Matlock. He lay stretched out, a hand pointing towards the cabinet. A sticky mass of blood had welled around his head.

Glenn broke into a run and slid to a halt on his side by his father. He cradled his father's head in his hands, but the head lolled and the deep hollow and matted blood that marred his father's grey hair should have told him instantly that he was dead.

But that truth didn't penetrate into his mind and he babbled incoherently as he urged him to get up. When his father just lay there, he stood and even walked him around, but his father's feet scraped over the floor, his arms slack, his weight a burden. At some point, Glenn was aware of someone looking through the door at him and he screeched at this man to get help. Then he returned to pacing back and forth, but slowly the truth of what had happened descended on him and he gently placed the body of his father on the floor, then hurried outside.

He ran over the hill, not even remembering to mount the bay, and charged down to Black Rock, his breath coming in pained wheezes as if he couldn't get enough air into his lungs. His head buzzed with a desperate desire for it to be half an hour earlier, when he'd been so happy trying to negotiate a few extra dollars for the cabinet. He'd have even traded another beating from Myron for how he felt now.

With his arms wheeling, he hurried past the first buildings and into the deserted main road. He'd now registered that the man who had looked in on him had been Myron and he would have had the sense to alert Doc Brown. So that left his sister Katie as the most important person for him to see.

On the boardwalk outside Bill's mercantile he slid to a halt, then stood for a moment composing himself and rehearsing the words that would destroy her life; then he pushed through the door.

Katie stood before the counter, Bill Cooke holding her shoulders as she stared at a spot just in front of her feet. Bill tensed and his action forced her to raise her head and look at Glenn, her eyes wide and pleading. She shrugged away from Bill and backed away until she slammed into the counter, a hand rising in a warding-off gesture.

'Stay away,' she murmured.

'I'm sorry,' Glenn blurted out, fighting down a sudden burst of anger, which he reckoned probably came because he hadn't been the one who had broken the terrible news to her. 'It's true. Someone's killed him.'

'Someone?'

'Yeah.' Glenn transferred his anger into a firm slap of a fist into his palm. 'But I'll find him and make him pay. You see that I do.'

'Someone?' she murmured again, then looked at

Bill, who urged her to stand behind him, but she pushed him away and faced Glenn. 'Myron says *you* killed pa.'

'Me?' Glenn murmured, backing away an involuntary pace. 'Why would he say that?'

'I . . . I don't know. I guess it's ridiculous, but Pa's drinking has been getting worse and you and he have been arguing again.' She shrugged. 'I guess I just don't know what to believe. . . .'

Glenn closed his eyes, fighting down a giddiness that threatened to brim over into nausea.

'Believe this. I only argued with him about his drinking because I love him. I didn't kill him.' With his eyes still closed he searched his memory for an image of what Myron might have seen, then shrugged. 'I was shocked. I guess I might have been crying and shouting and walking him around. He might have thought we were fighting. It was dark inside and he didn't stay long. I guess . . . I guess. . . .'

He opened his eyes and held his hands wide, imploring her to understand.

'I believe you.' She gave a tense smile. 'They must have killed him for . . .'

She glanced at Bill then lowered her head.

'For what?' Glenn asked.

Katie opened her mouth to reply, but before she could say anything, the door crashed open behind Glenn and the sudden darkness that descended on the room gave Glenn the impression that several people were standing around the doorway.

Katie shook her head as she looked over Glenn's shoulder.

'Not now.' She hurried across the room to stand beside him. 'Stay out of the way while I explain what happened.'

Glenn still didn't look at the door, although he heard murmuring behind him and detected Myron's grunted tones along with those of several others.

'Hiding behind you will just convince them I'm guilty. I'll talk to them.'

Glenn moved to turn, but Katie placed a hand on his arm and gripped him tightly.

'Myron is here,' she murmured from the corner of her mouth. 'He's mighty angry and he's all set to hand out justice. He said you'd been looking for a fight and you have it coming to you. Run, it's for the best. I'll make them understand. You just run. Just run.'

Glenn listened to the steady clump of footfalls approaching from behind. Then Myron grunted a warning to step away from his sister.

Either he stayed to explain what had happened, or he ran and let Katie explain. But one look at her pleading expression convinced him that being else-where at this moment was the better idea. He clamped a hand on her arm and held on to her.

'But once you've explained, I will find out who did this. I promise.'

She patted his hand and, with that, he ran for the back exit and did as she'd urged. He ran. And ran. They chased him out of the mercantile and then the town, Myron in the lead and goading on a growing trail of townsfolk with his conviction that he'd seen Glenn murder his father.

When he eventually escaped Katie couldn't explain away what had happened and, as it turned out, running *was* the worst thing he could have done. It convinced even the most doubting of people of his guilt and, no matter what she said in his defence, the townsfolk talked themselves into a state where they were angry enough to hire Randall Nash to find him.

And when Randall found Glenn and dragged him back to town, that anger almost resulted in their lynching him.

Glenn shook himself, freeing his mind from dwelling yet again on those terrible events. He looked at Randall, the man who had caught him and brought him back to Black Rock the first time. But Randall wasn't looking at him. His eyes were peering all around while he kept his head directed towards the approaching creek.

'Is someone following us?' Glenn asked, his anger at recalling those events making his voice husky. 'You've done that before. You don't move your head, but your eyes look everywhere.'

'You're an observant man,' Randall said, hunching forwards in the saddle, 'and to answer your question, we *are* being followed, but don't go thinking a rescue is a-coming. It's Arnold Jameson.'

'Who's he?'

'A fellow bounty hunter, but he ain't got the morals I got.'

Glenn snorted. 'That's hard to believe.'

'Even amongst men who ain't got morals, some men have even less than the others, and Arnold Jameson is such a man. I saw him hanging around

Leavenworth and I got him talking, and he sure did grumble about having to wait a week to pick you up.'

'Yeah. They said there was a problem and I had to stay another week.' Glenn shrugged. 'So you decided to get to me first?'

'Sure did. And it was lucky for you Arnold drank too much whiskey the night before they let you go.' Randall laughed. 'Or, he didn't taste the something I had put in his whiskey until he woke up too late to collect you.'

'And that's moral?'

'I was just thinking of you. You wouldn't have enjoyed your journey to Black Rock so much with Arnold.' Randall nodded back and Glenn turned to see that Arnold was leading two other riders in towards the trail. All the men had their guns drawn and were speeding up as they closed on them. 'And it's my job to make sure you keep on enjoying yourself with me.'

CHAPTER 3

'Free my hands,' Glenn shouted over the rapid beating of the pounding hoofs.

'I ain't releasing you so you can run,' Randall said.

Glenn glanced over his shoulder and saw that the man Randall had identified as Arnold Jameson and the other riders were closing with every stride. Now they were just a hundred yards back.

'Then you can release me when Arnold takes me from you.'

Randall firmed his jaw, then pointed ahead and barked instructions for the quickest way of fording the creek. Glenn returned a nod, but he had no intention of heading across it.

He had to seize any chance for escape that came his way, and as they were less than fours hours from Black Rock, he judged this distraction to be his last chance. With both Randall and now Arnold after him, it was a slim chance, but still the best he could have hoped for.

So when they waded into the water, Glenn kept abreast of Randall until the water lapped at his horse's belly. Then he drew back slightly, letting Randall take the lead in finding the shallowest route.

He glanced over his shoulder, seeing that Arnold was now ahead of the other two men as they splashed into the shallows. But when he turned back he saw movement further down the creek. Four more men were galloping along the edge of the water, aiming to cut them off on the other side of the creek.

'They were waiting for us,' he shouted, 'we got no chance.'

'Just keep going,' Randall shouted and surged on ahead, but Glenn pulled back hard on the reins, halting his horse, then turned.

His mount reared in the water. With his hands tied together, Glenn struggled to control it, but then it bounded on ahead. Glenn enjoyed several moments where ahead was the open creek and freedom and he almost dared to imagine he might escape. Then his luck gave out. The horse hurtled into a deeper stretch of water and, without traction, his steed floundered. With his hands slick and tied, he was unable to keep himself upright. He slipped from the saddle and fell headlong into the water.

Randall was still heading away from him and bearing down on the four riders on the other side of the creek. Arnold and the other two men were spreading out, ready to surround him. So Glenn resolved to swim to safety. He kicked off from the river-bed, then swam downriver, thrusting forward with just his legs, but he managed only three strokes before he reached the end of the deeper stretch of water and his knees scraped across stones. He stood and hurled himself through the water as, from behind him, he heard Randall then Arnold shout out a warning.

Glenn ignored them, concentrating on running at an angle to Arnold, who pranced his horse through the water, aiming to cut him off. Arnold gained on him with every pace, his speed great enough to ensure that he was certain to run him down before Glenn reached dry land.

Glenn hurried on, knowing his escape attempt was futile but hoping for a stroke of luck as he threw himself forward. He did succeed in reaching the shallower water before Arnold bore down on him. Arnold released a length of rope, then played it out before swinging it overhead in a circle, gradually lengthening his swings until, as he flanked Glenn, he hurled the rope.

But as the rope came down over Glenn's head and tightened around his chest, Randall's rifle shot cracked, the sound echoing. Arnold hurtled backwards from his horse to land in the shallow water. His momentum yanked Glenn to his knees. Even while the ripples were still spreading from Arnold's body, Randall fired at the other two men.

As these men dragged their horses to a halt, Glenn rolled to his feet and struggled to free himself from the coils of rope. He watched the men draw their guns, then darted his gaze to the side to watch Randall defiantly keep his horse square in the centre of the creek. Randall slammed his rifle to his shoulder and took aim with deadly speed and accuracy. He peeled off two crisp shots, both hitting their targets and crashing the men from their horses. Then he swirled round to face the other men on the other side of the creek.

Stranded in the open water and with the sustained gunfire spooking their mounts, these men's returning fire was wild. After only one volley of gunshots they panicked and split up, two men heading off in either direction.

Glenn at last managed to drag the lasso over his head, then hurried to Arnold's horse, which was now standing on the edge of the water and idly appraising developments.

As he reached the horse another burst of gunfire ripped out behind him. He glanced back to see that Randall was ignoring him. Instead, he was still heading across the creek, aiming to cut down the distance on the fleeing men. He reached the other side of the water and jumped down from his horse to stand on dry land. There, he threw himself to the ground to come to rest on his belly with the rifle aimed up.

One carefully directed shot tore the nearest straggler from his horse. Then Randall jumped up to kneel on one knee and take aim at the other men. These men had all scattered and were hurrying away, their horses kicking up their heels as the riders showed no sign of returning to try another attack.

On the other side of the creek, Glenn secured the reins of Arnold's horse while he heard Randall continue to fire speculative shots at the fleeing men. Then he saw movement in the water nearby. He glanced to the side to see Arnold rolling to his knees. Glenn had assumed that Randall had fatally wounded him, but as Arnold got to his feet, Glenn saw he had only received a shoulder nick. And he was out of Randall's line of sight. Arnold staggered to his feet clutching his bleeding shoulder, then drew his gun and sighted Randall's back.

'Randall, watch out!' Glenn shouted without thinking, but Randall didn't react as he continued to blast slugs at the fleeing men.

Glenn glanced at the open creek ahead, judging he might be able to outrun whichever one of them survived this gunfight. But as he moved to mount the horse he saw the cold metal dangling from Arnold's saddle – the chains with which he had planned to bind him.

He made a sudden decision.

He grabbed the chains, turned to face Arnold, then swung them round his head twice and released them. The chains gleamed as they rose, catching the rays of the sun, then arced downwards with deadly accuracy. Arnold had just thrust his arm out, ready to shoot Randall in the back, but then flinched when he noticed the approaching missile.

But he was too late. The chains clipped his forehead, spinning him into the water, an agonized screech tearing from his lips. This time, Randall swirled round and was just in time to see Arnold roll to a halt.

Glenn once again looked at the expanse of meandering creek ahead, weighing up his chances of escaping a determined and practised manhunter like Randall. He judged his chances to be low, but he also judged that Randall would now be grateful enough to release him. So he led Arnold's horse back down

27

the side of the creek to join Randall when he waded back through the creek.

Randall stood over Arnold's supine body, then looked up at Glenn and tipped his hat, smiling with genuine delight for the first time Glenn had seen.

Together they dragged Arnold from the water and deposited him on dry land. Then Randall stood on the edge of the water, raised a foot on to a boulder, and sighted Arnold down the barrel of his rifle.

With his eyes rolling and unfocused, Arnold peered up at him.

'Put that other hand high where I can see it,' Randall grunted, 'and you'll get to live.'

Arnold winced, then rolled to his knees and feet. He did put a hand high, but then lowered it to clutch his bloodied shoulder.

Randall gestured for him to kneel, then frisked him, discarding a hidden gun. By the time he'd finished his search Arnold was swaying and when Randall stood back and signified he should hold out his hands to be tied up, he keeled over on to his side.

'I must have hurt him real bad,' Glenn said, joining him.

Randall snorted. 'You didn't. Men like Arnold act tough, but when it comes down to it, they bawl like a baby over a mere nick.'

He tapped his boot against Arnold's chest, producing a groan, then turned to Glenn and smiled.

Glenn returned the smile. 'Guess I'm glad I chose to help you, after all.'

'And I'm obliged for your help. That took some skill to hit him with those chains.'

Glenn shrugged. 'In Leavenworth you had to improvise.'

'I'll remember that.' Randall widened his smile to a grin, then let a deep frown emerge. 'But I'd still be obliged if you'd put your hands high. Your free time is over.' Randall swung his rifle round to sight Glenn's chest. 'Did you enjoy it?'

'My free time is . . .' Glenn slapped his thigh. 'I just saved your life and you're still taking me in.'

'That's what I do. I'm a bounty hunter. I don't take sides. I just take 'em in for the bounty.'

'You . . . You . . .'

'Double-crossing snake?' Randall watched Glenn grunt his agreement, then chuckled. 'Now put those hands high or you'll get what Arnold got.'

Glenn eventually found his voice and treated Randall to a torrent of abuse, but Randall waited until his hoarse voice petered out. Then he ordered him to sit while he turned his ministrations to Arnold.

The wounded man was still lying on his side, groaning, and when Randall dragged him into a sitting position he looked back at him through half-open eyes, the globes white.

'You fine now you've rested?' Randall asked.

'Go to hell,' Arnold murmured, swaying.

'Don't worry. I *will* get you to a sawbones and get you all fixed up. But that depends on whether you co-operate. So tell me everything.'

Arnold's eyes flickered and he slumped to the side, but Randall grabbed him to stop him falling, then shook him. Arnold shivered as he focused his eyes on Randall.

'About what?' he murmured, his voice low and weak.

'About all the things you wouldn't tell me in Leavenworth. About how you got to hear about Glenn Price. About why a two-hundred-and-fifty-dollar bounty interests you so much. About what you've learned so far about the man who actually killed Myron Cole. And about anything else you'd care to tell me.'

'I got nothing to say about nothing until I get fixed up.' Arnold's jaw quivered, but he managed a defiant grin. 'And even then, I'll never talk to the likes of you.'

'That means you do know something, and you'll tell me what it is unless you want to bake some more in the sun. Now tell me – who killed Myron Cole?'

'Kill Myron. . . .' Arnold's eyes flashed with some emotion, perhaps humour. Then they rolled up and he fell over on to his side.

'Randall,' Glenn urged, 'despite what you've been doing to me, you ain't a cruel man. You got to get him some help.'

'He's pretending. I only nicked his shoulder.'

'And I hit his head. I reckon he's hurt real bad.'

'Be quiet. I'll do the reckoning here.'

This time Glenn did as ordered and Randall settled down to await the pain working its persuasive power on Arnold. But as the sun rose higher in the sky until it beat down on them, Glenn became increasingly determined to make Randall listen to him.

Arnold wouldn't come conscious for more than a minute and each time, his eyes rolled up and he collapsed again. Glenn had hit him a glancing blow to the head and so, when Arnold was again unconscious, he shuffled over to him and fingered his scalp.

Sure enough, within the greasy hair, he found matted blood and a deep scrape. Glenn knew that head wounds often didn't bleed much but that they could still be fatal. He pointed this out to Randall, who, with much grumbling, at last relented from his attempt to wait Arnold out.

He bound his hands, dragged him to his horse, and threw him over the saddle. Throughout, Arnold uttered only the shallowest of groans.

Glenn stood back, watching them.

'Come on,' Randall said to Glenn. 'I'm doing what you wanted and getting him to a doctor.'

Glenn glanced around. In the confusion of the gunfight the horse he'd been riding had galloped off, as had the other horses.

'And how am I supposed to get there?'

Randall secured Glenn with a rope around his waist then led him to his own horse.

'You get to walk behind us.'

Glenn sighed. 'I just had to ask.'

CHAPTER 4

The nearly full moon was rising into the twilit sky by the time Randall pulled up outside Doc Brown's house with the footsore and roped Glenn trundling along behind. The house was a quarter-mile from the towering finger of black rock and around five miles out of the town of Black Rock and so, despite his weariness, Glenn hoped this distraction had delayed his return to town until tomorrow.

Randall dragged Arnold from his horse. Arnold's breathing was fitful and he was murmuring under his breath; his red face was clammy. Randall let him lie on the ground while he released Glenn. Then, still holding on to Glenn's rope, he and Glenn carried the semi-conscious man into the house.

As they headed inside, Glenn couldn't help but wince when he saw the blood that was dribbling from a corner of Arnold's mouth. Sure enough, Doc Brown only took one look at Arnold before he winced too, then directed Randall to place him on a table.

The doctor touched his neck while he lifted an

eyelid, frowning. When he released him, Arnold's head rolled back. While the doctor busied himself with collecting his equipment, Randall tugged on Glenn's rope and signified that he should sit with his back to the wall.

As Glenn moved to comply, Brown glanced at him, then at Randall.

'Who's that you got with you?' he asked.

'Surprised you don't recognize him,' Randall said. 'He used to live in Black Rock.'

Brown placed his black bag on the table beside Arnold, then considered Glenn. He narrowed his eyes, then widened them with a start, but Glenn spoke up before he could confirm that he recognized him.

'Doc Brown, I remember you as being a decent man and whether you believe I did what everyone says I did or not, know this – I've served my time and I'm innocent of what Randall reckons I did this time.' Glenn stood and tugged on his rope, giving himself enough leeway to stand away from Randall and let him face the doctor. 'He's got no right holding me but he's gone and done it anyhow.'

Brown rubbed his jaw, then blew out his cheeks.

'You finished?'

'I have, aside from the fact that if you check out my story, you'll see I have the best alibi a man could want for not doing anything Randall says I've done.'

'Interesting.' Brown turned to Randall and smiled. 'You sure do bring in the interesting ones.'

'Like it always has been, Alan,' Randall said. 'And like it always will be.'

Glenn slumped to his knees.

'You two are friends,' he murmured, crestfallen.

'We sure are,' Brown said.

'And,' Randall said as he slapped a firm hand on Glenn's shoulder and pushed him back to a sitting position, 'you picked the wrong man to bleat to, so I'll be talking to you about that later.'

Brown chuckled under his breath as he opened his bag and laid out a row of knives and probes on the table.

'You wasted your breath on me, Glenn,' he said. 'I don't care who's done right or who's done wrong. If Sheriff Price reckons Randall has to bring you in, that's good enough for me.'

'Why won't nobody take sides or listen to me?' Glenn murmured then looked up, but Brown had turned his back on him and, with Randall turning his back on him too, he found that he was talking to himself.

'What's this one done?' Brown asked, prodding Arnold's elbow then working up to his shoulder.

'Tried to steal my prisoner. I'd be obliged if you can get him talking.'

Brown considered Arnold, then leaned over him and parted his hair, murmuring to himself.

'I'll get him talking as soon as I can, but he won't be doing that any time soon. This man has had a severe blow to the head.'

Randall nodded and sat on the edge of Brown's table.

'Then what about you? What do you know about Myron Cole's death?'

'Not much.' Brown opened his bag and removed a small bottle.

Randall rubbed his chin, considering. 'But could somebody have taken revenge against a man who put a member of the Price family in jail?'

Brown paused from fussing over Arnold for long enough to utter a derisive snort.

'Things never change much in Black Rock. The Archer family still opposes the Prices, but nobody listens to them any more. And nobody cares for Glenn either. They tried to lynch him fifteen years ago and there's more chance of someone trying to do that again than anybody taking revenge on his behalf.'

Brown smiled and Randall considered the smile, then offered one of his own.

'You may not know anything, but I reckon you got an idea.'

'Just a rumination. Three months ago old Adam Price died. The town needed a new mayor and Myron Cole decided to stand against Clyde Price.'

'You saying the Prices killed him?'

'Not saying nothing. It was just mighty convenient for them he died and now Clyde is sure to become the new mayor. And everybody says the new blood will strengthen the grip that family has on Black Rock.'

'Either way, I'm getting to hear the Price name too often for my liking.'

Brown nodded then shooed Randall away.

'Now, keep quiet and keep out of way, I got a bullet wound to dress and some serious thinking to do about this head wound.'

Randall pushed himself off the table and took a pace towards the nearest open door.

'We'll wait in your other room.'

Brown flinched, then shook his head.

'Give me room and peace by waiting in the barn.'

Randall edged to the side to peer into the other room.

'You got chairs in there and—'

'And I don't want that Price in my house any longer than I have to. Take him to the barn.' Brown darted a finger at Glenn then at the door. Then he sighed and replaced his stern expression and sudden burst of anger with a smile. 'Just secure him in the barn. You can wait in here, but he can't.'

Randall stayed long enough to watch Brown start work, then led Glenn outside.

'Seems you ain't welcome anywhere,' he said as he led him to the barn.

'I ain't welcome in Black Rock, that's for sure.'

'That mean you're welcome elsewhere with friends who'd help you?'

'Yeah, that's . . .' Glenn snorted as Randall pushed him through the barn door, then he swirled round. 'You're trying to get me to admit I got friends who'd help me out. And perhaps I have, but they aren't in Black Rock and I sure didn't get anyone to kill Myron Cole.'

'As you've said.' Randall secured him to the central post in the barn, then paced three steps away and considered him with his arms folded. 'Arnold's distraction has bought you one last night to think things through, but if you don't do yourself some mighty sensible thinking, tomorrow I'll be taking you in to Black Rock and then—'

Outside, a gunshot blasted, the noise near but muffled. Then another shot and a raised voice sounded. Randall darted his gaze around the barn, confirming that Glenn was the only person there, then rechecked his bonds and headed to the barn door. He stayed to the side of the door then ventured a glance around it.

Glenn edged to the side to the maximum extent of his rope to let him see what was happening outside. Presently he saw a rider hurtle by. The man fired sideways, his wild shot tearing through the open barn door before scything into the dirt ten feet to Glenn's side.

Glenn scurried for safety behind the post as Randall hurried outside, skidded to a halt, then tore off several quick shots at the fleeing rider. But he quickly desisted and sped to his horse, his downcast gaze and firm-set jaw confirming Glenn's sighting as the rider had hurtled by the barn door.

Arnold Jameson had just escaped.

At sun-up Doc Brown provided Glenn and Randall with breakfast in the barn.

Glenn again tried to convince the doctor that Randall had no good reason to take him in to Black Rock, but Brown refused even to enter into conversation with him, so Glenn relented.

Instead, Brown and Randall discussed the events of last night. Brown's embarrassed gaze rarely met

Randall's and their sparse chat avoided giving Glenn too many details, but from the snippets of conversation he overheard, Glenn pieced together what had happened.

Even before Doc Brown had dressed Arnold's shoulder wound, Arnold had come to faster than his demeanour of the last few hours had suggested he could. He had knocked out the doctor, then escaped. Randall had pursued him, but returned within the hour, the thick clouds that had spread across the night sky until they obscured the moon not letting him follow Arnold's trail in the dark.

From the gruff tone in the voices of both men as they discussed these events, Glenn judged that Randall didn't blame Brown and that this setback wouldn't threaten their friendship. In fact both men were worried about the other's reaction to an uncomfortable situation.

When they'd eaten Brown returned to his house, and he didn't emerge when they prepared to move out. Glenn also reckoned that Brown wasn't to blame, as clearly Arnold had been more devious than Randall had given him credit for, but Randall's firm jaw and narrowed eyes suggested to Glenn that commenting on this wouldn't be taken well.

Accordingly, Glenn said nothing as Randall again secured him and made him walk behind his horse.

Glenn stayed quiet as they headed to the trail and later rode alongside the rail-tracks as they approached Black Rock. Glenn was mentally preparing himself for a homecoming he never thought he'd have to suffer when, two miles out of town,

Randall veered to the side and then proceeded up a hill.

With a start, Glenn realized where they were heading.

'What you going to my home for?' he asked.

'I'm giving you that last chance to tell me something interesting before you can start panicking.'

'I got no . . .'

Glenn gulped. Ahead of him, his old home was edging into view from behind the rounded hill that he and Katie had often run up and down when he was younger. He'd never expected, or wanted, to see this place again, but now that he had, a bitter combination of memories and regret assailed him, the acrid taste of bile rising in his throat. He could do nothing but stare at the approaching building, trying to imagine it as it had been before fifteen years of neglect had destroyed it.

On a patch of bare earth before the ruined house, Randall dismounted and Glenn followed him through the gap that had once been a door. The roof had long gone, the roof timbers being more valuable and so more worth stealing than the small amount of furniture they'd possessed. And sure enough the remnants of that furniture still littered the floor, smashed and rotted beyond recognition.

'You look thoughtful,' Randall said, without a trace of mockery in his tone.

'Yeah,' Glenn said. 'I left this place after finding Pa's body and I haven't been back since.'

'Then the memories will be as fresh as they ever were. Tell me what happened. Leave nothing out, and if it includes something that tells me who killed Myron Cole, you can go.'

Glenn looked at Randall, seeing in his blank expression no malice towards him and perhaps a promise that he wouldn't double-cross him.

'I'd gone to see Matlock Langhorne and when I came back, I found my father lying dead, just there.' Glenn pointed at a spot four feet from a crumbling inner wall.

Randall paced across the room then looked up. Glenn directed him to move two paces forward until he was standing on the spot where he had stood fifteen years ago.

Randall hunkered down, fingering the dirt, then looked around.

'Home must have looked mighty different then.'

'Yeah. There was a cabinet to your side. Father had built it and was mighty proud of it.'

Randall looked at the heap of rotted wood to his left.

'Looks like there's a smashed table here and maybe chairs there, but no cabinet.'

Glenn shrugged. 'Somebody must have stolen it.'

'Perhaps they did. What else do you remember?'

'Nothing. I found him lying dead where you're kneeling with his head smashed in. I came over, cradled his head, got blood all over me, and Myron saw me. He ran off to town, and I followed to tell Katie what I'd found, but Myron had told everyone I'd killed him. I told Katie he was wrong, but Myron had worked everyone up, and I ran.'

'You ran,' Randall intoned. 'And you kept on

running until I found you.'

'Running doesn't mean I was guilty.'

'But what Myron said did. He said you and John were fighting and that you were laughing as you killed him.'

Glenn paced round on the spot to look towards town. Myron's smithy was close to the tracks, just out of his view. He searched for any hatred of Myron for telling what at the time had sounded like spiteful lies, but found none. He had been in shock when he'd found the body and he found it hard to recall all his actions, and he guessed it might have been the same for Myron.

'I got no idea what he might have thought he saw and heard.'

'Why did he come here?'

'Don't know.'

'And your feelings when you found the body?'

'I was shocked, if that's what you mean.' Glenn paced back and forth and when he spoke it was more to himself than to Randall. 'Katie and me came out to Black Rock on the orphan train. We were supposed to go to god-fearing families and we almost went to Adam Price.'

'Perhaps things might have been different if you had.'

'Yeah, Adam hadn't had children but then his wife died and he remarried. She gave him children: Clyde and then Emerson, but like his brother's first wife, John's wife couldn't provide children and that had soured them both. And when she died, he turned to drink. But we still loved him and hoped he'd come

41

out of the bad times.'

'And who do you reckon killed him?'

'No idea. We had no enemies and we had nothing to steal.'

'Except a cabinet that your father died beside.'

'Yeah, but . . .' Glenn narrowed his eyes. 'What you saying?'

'Perhaps somebody wanted the cabinet, or what was in the cabinet.'

'There was nothing in . . .' Glenn shrugged then paced across the room to stand beside Randall. He hunkered down, taking the position he had assumed fifteen years ago and trying to envisage that day. A flashed memory came to him of him kneeling here and he nodded. 'The cabinet door had swung open, and he lay with a hand pointing towards it.'

He looked up at Randall, hoping he'd say something else that'd jog his fading memory of that day. Clues as to who had killed his father were locked away in his mind and perhaps would never emerge. And as if to taunt him even more, that long-suppressed need to find who was responsible was hammering at his mind again.

'Anything?' Randall asked, his question snapping Glenn out of his pondering.

'No, and I guess nothing will ever come to me if this place can't drag it out.'

Randall nodded, an emotion flashing in his eyes, perhaps regret.

'Then I got no choice but to take you in.'

Randall grabbed his arm and led him through the door. At first, the shock of revisiting his former home had numbed Glenn, but when they reached the horse, he struggled.

In response Randall gripped him even more tightly and checked his bonds.

'Don't do this, Randall,' Glenn said.

'Got no choice.'

'You got plenty. You must want something more than a mere two hundred and fifty dollars. Is that worth a man's life? Stand up for something more than just—'

'Quit babbling!' Randall roared, raising a hand as if to strike Glenn. Then he lowered his hand, a twitch contorting his features as if he really did hate the thought of mistreating a prisoner, or perhaps he did feel regret for what he was about to do.

With Glenn staying quiet, he mounted up. At a steady pace, they headed down the side of the hill to ride alongside the tracks.

Glenn kept his head down as they swung past Myron's smithy. There were no more buildings before they'd reach Black Rock and Glenn didn't hold out much hope that he would go unnoticed for much longer.

'I ain't babbling, Randall,' he said, 'when I say I'm innocent.'

'Not my problem,' Randall said, not looking back. 'I'm no lawman, I just—'

'—bring 'em in for the bounty.' Glenn struggled against his bonds, but found no give and had no choice but to desist. 'But even if you don't care about me, you got to admit that taking me into town, hoping my presence will shake the truth out of someone, is looking for trouble.'

'Yeah. And I never shy away from that.'

At a walking pace they soon closed on the first buildings and, as the town opened up before him, Glenn saw that it had expanded in the years while he had been away. The railroad had arrived a year before he'd gone to jail, and back then the town had been bursting out in all directions, rough buildings going up with frantic speed. Now, the town had the solid and quiet authority his father had reckoned it would have one day.

But each pace nearer town helped to destroy Glenn's last lingering hopes that Randall wouldn't take him into a town where the townsfolk had once tried to lynch him.

'What you reckon Sheriff Price will do with me?' he asked, voicing his concern despite his determination not to.

'Arrest you,' Randall said, without turning. 'Then you'll get your day in court, like last time.'

'And what chance did I have then? Adam Price picked the jury, and Judge Mitchell was in his pay.'

'Adam spoke up for you. If he hadn't, you'd have swung.'

'Fifteen years in Leavenworth for a crime I didn't commit don't make me feel right disposed to my adoptive family's memory.'

'And Myron Cole?'

'You won't let this go, will you? I am an innocent man. I was breaking rocks when Myron Cole died and there ain't no way you can explain that fact away.'

Randall shrugged. 'You may not have pulled the trigger, but perhaps you got someone else to do it.'

'Perhaps, you said *perhaps*. Up until now you've said I did it or you don't care, but now I reckon you're having second thoughts about this. Don't—'

'Be quiet!' Randall snorted his breath, then gestured at the first building, now just twenty paces ahead of them. 'This is your last chance, Glenn, for you to tell me what you know.'

'I've told you everything I know.'

'Then tell me what you don't know.'

'What you mean?'

Randall turned in the saddle to look down at Glenn while still riding on. Urgency quickened his voice as he barked his demands.

'I mean start talking. If you don't know who killed your father fifteen years ago and why somebody has now killed the principal witness, then tell me about other things. Tell me what you suspect. Tell me who hated other people. Tell me something, anything, but unless you give me a clue, I'm heading into Black Rock.'

Glenn searched his memory, hoping to come up with something that'd intrigue Randall, but his mind remained resolutely blank.

'I can't help you,' he whispered.

Randall flashed a harsh smile then turned in the saddle and yanked on Glenn's rope, dragging him on.

'Then I reckon this is one homecoming you won't enjoy.'

45

CHAPTER 5

Randall continued riding at a sedate pace until he reached the main road, then tipped his hat to a man standing on the end of the boardwalk.

The man nodded to Randall, then looked at Glenn with wide-eyed bemusement, but Glenn judged the man to be too young to remember him. But as they swung round to head down the main road he saw that dozens of people were going about their business in the bustling town. Although he didn't recognize anyone in his brief review of these people, somebody was sure to recognize him before long.

To postpone that inevitable moment, Glenn lowered his head, hoping the passage of fifteen years and the sheer unlikeliness of his returning would keep his identity hidden.

With his hat pulled low he could see people only up to their waists. From the corner of his eye he noticed that everyone they passed stopped to watch him, then followed them down the road. The crowd grew in size, murmuring amongst themselves and watching with the excitement that any crowd would have when they saw a man being led into town in bonds.

Then a child swung into view. The freckle-faced, grinning youngster peered up at him, then scurried off to report what he looked like to his friends. None of the adults was so bold as to approach him and Glenn started counting the paces until he reached the sheriff's office.

Then footfalls pattered behind him and someone tapped him on the small of the back. With his head thrust down even further, Glenn turned, but he faced another child. He flashed a snarling grimace that rocked the child back on his heels before he scampered away, but then Randall's steady advancing pulled his rope taut and tugged him.

While turning he let the rope pull him forward, but then he stumbled. With a start he realized that the tap on the back had been a distraction and that another child had silently slipped around him, then bent over in his path to trip him over. But the prank worked and Glenn fell over the boy and tumbled all his length, then had to fight to regain his footing while Randall continued to drag him down the road.

He resumed his walking as chortling erupted from the child who had obviously won a dare, but that was of no concern to Glenn. The damage had already been done. He had shown his face to everyone.

Then the talking started.

'I recognize him,' someone announced. 'That's . . . that's . . .'

'Glenn Price,' another voice said.

'It can't be,' a third voice said.

'It is. I tell you. Glenn Price is in town again.'

'But he got life in Leavenworth.'

'He got fifteen years. And ... And, yeah, John Price died fifteen years ago.'

'And he's being dragged into town again.'

'That's because he ain't learnt his lesson. He's just as loco as he always was.'

Glenn was hurried on as the comments grew in intensity and more people started to convince themselves that they knew his identity.

Randall glanced to his side at the rising clamour, then urged his horse on. With minimal fuss he dismounted outside the sheriff's office. He then headed across the boardwalk towards the door.

By now people were milling in. Randall had to barge several people out of the way to reach the door and when Glenn slipped in through the door, those people formed a solid barrier outside it.

As the door slammed shut and Glenn became accustomed to the darkened interior, he glanced through the only window to see the crowd line up on the boardwalk and peer in. Then he turned to see Sheriff Emerson Price standing before him, his slouched stance and thin-lipped smile displaying none of the surprise everyone outside had shown.

'Glenn Price,' he murmured. 'I ain't pleased to see you again.'

Glenn glanced at Randall, but Randall held his hand out, inviting him to speak.

'Emerson,' Glenn said, 'I know you and I didn't exactly get on before, but you got to listen to me. I

48

got plenty to say and you got to hear me out.'

Emerson glared at Glenn, his upper lip curled in distaste, then looked at Randall.

'You've done Black Rock a great service by bringing in this varmint. Can't believe many bounty hunters have brought in the same man twice.'

Randall snorted a laugh then turned to look at the row of faces pressing in at the window. He headed to the window and closed the shutters, then turned back.

'I guess not, and even for two hundred and fifty dollars, it was worth it.'

'The bounty has gone up to five hundred. I now have evidence he gunned down Myron Cole.'

'Hey,' Glenn shouted, tugging on his rope, but Randall stood before him.

'Like Glenn was about to say,' he said, 'he didn't shoot Myron. He might know something about his death, but he didn't actually shoot him.'

'That ain't right,' Emerson said, shaking his head. 'You see, I got a witness who saw Glenn kill Myron.'

'You can't believe that—' Glenn shouted before Randall raised a hand, silencing him.

'What did this *witness* see, exactly?' Randall asked, narrowing his eyes.

'The details are for the court, but it all fits in. Glenn just had enough time to leave jail, head here, and kill Myron in revenge for his damning testimony.'

Randall shook his head. 'You got that wrong, Sheriff. Glenn has been in my custody ever since they kicked him out of Leavenworth.'

'He must have had some free time. It wouldn't take you ten days to get here.'

'It took me *three* days. Glenn got out of jail a week late.'

Emerson winced. 'A week late. . . ?'

'Yeah. He's got plenty to answer for, but he sure didn't shoot Myron. It seems you got a bigger mystery here than you first thought.' Randall tugged Glenn forward, then pushed him towards Emerson. 'Reckon as you need to keep him safe while you work out what it all means.'

Emerson shuffled from foot to foot. 'You sure he was a week late in leaving jail?'

'Yeah. There was some problem with his paperwork, but I waited and picked him up the moment he left.'

Emerson turned to look at the shuttered windows. He lowered his voice.

'Anybody else know about this?'

'Aside from Arnold. . . .' Randall snorted his breath. 'What you saying?'

'I'm saying Glenn ain't exactly popular here. Most people reckon we should have lynched him fifteen years ago.' Emerson looked Glenn up and down and smirked. 'I reckon we have enough on him now to finish the job.'

'You haven't. He could have hired someone to kill Myron, but he didn't kill him. You need real evidence of that before you start talking about hanging a man.'

'I got a witness.'

'A badly informed witness.'

'But still a witness.'

As Randall scratched the back of his head, Emerson slapped a hand on Glenn's rope and dragged him forward.

'The law ain't doing this to me again,' Glenn muttered. 'I'm innocent.'

'You ain't innocent,' Emerson grunted.

'Emerson, whatever you think of me, I'm still a Price. Don't do this.'

'You ain't no real Price. The closest you ever came to Price blood is when you spilled it.'

Glenn considered Emerson's sneering expression, seeing the bloodlust burning his eyes, and the bared teeth that said there was no possibility of mercy here or that he had any interest in uncovering who had really killed Myron. He had heard the truth he wanted to hear and no matter what anyone said, he'd stick with that truth until Glenn was swinging.

Glenn swirled round to face Randall.

'You wanted to shake the truth out by bringing me here, Randall,' he screeched as Emerson dragged him towards his desk. 'But Emerson doesn't want to hear that truth. He just wants an excuse, any excuse, to hang me. Do something.'

Emerson snorted. 'Randall's a bounty hunter. He just brings 'em in for the bounty. It ain't his concern what happens to them then.' While still holding on to Glenn's rope, Emerson went behind his desk and withdrew an envelope from the top drawer. 'There's a five-hundred-dollar bounty here for the service you've done to our town.'

'Randall,' Glenn shouted, 'that's blood-money and

that blood will be on your hands for ever. Don't take it. You're a fair man. You got to take a stand now.'

Randall stared at the floor for a moment, then paced across the room to stand beside Glenn. He held out a hand and, with a sly grin, Emerson slipped the bills from the envelope and placed them on Randall's palm. Instead of closing his hand around them, Randall snapped the hand up, sending the bills flying. Then he followed through with a round-armed club to Emerson's jaw with his other hand, wheeling the sheriff over his desk.

Emerson landed with a clatter and a grunted cry on the other side. Glenn felt his rope go slack as Randall peered over the desk, seeing, like Glenn, that Emerson's head lolled before he rolled on his back to lie supine and sprawled.

Glenn breathed a sigh of relief. 'Obliged to you for—'

'Be quiet,' Randall snapped. 'I got to think about this.'

'You don't need to do no thinking. You just need to get us both out of here. If my no-good cousin is what passes for the law in Black Rock, I ain't the only one here who's going to get lynched.'

'Nobody will lynch me for that tap on the chin.'

'They will. Emerson hired Arnold to bring me in, except you got to me first, and Arnold wouldn't have cared that the evidence was a lie.' Glenn offered a hopeful smile. 'Arnold just ain't got the morals you got.'

Randall pointed at Emerson's unconscious form. 'You saying this lawman killed Myron?'

52

'Maybe, but at the very least, he knows who did do it and he's covering up for him and framing me to make me pay for what he thinks I did fifteen years ago.'

'Agreed on that.' Randall turned to the door. 'And I'm getting out of town.'

'*We* are getting out,' Glenn said, shuffling to the side to stand before Randall. He held out his bound hands. 'You brought me here and you got to get me out.'

Randall snorted and moved to walk past Glenn.

'You don't understand me, Glenn. This is your problem and it's far too complicated for me. Find your own way out of town.'

Glenn jumped to the side to block Randall's route again. He thrust out his hands to him.

'I *do* understand you and you're a fairer man than you'll admit. Get these ropes off me and we can get out of town more easily.'

'You don't order me around. And you got me wrong.' Randall barged past Glenn. 'I don't rescue nobody when there ain't no bounty involved.'

'Then,' Glenn said, raising his voice as he thrust out a leg to avoid falling, 'you're just as bad as Arnold Jameson.'

Randall reached for the door. 'Taunts won't work on me.'

'Then think about this,' Glenn snapped. 'I got more idea as to what's happening here than you have. And when there's this much going on, there's sure to be a bounty at the end of it. You'll need me to claim it.'

Randall stomped to a halt before the door. He

stood for a moment, then sighed and turned. Without further words, he extracted a knife from his boot and slit through Glenn's bonds, freeing his wrists.

As he slipped out from the rope and followed him to the door, Glenn stayed quiet, preferring not to risk Randall's changing his mind while his position was so precarious.

Outside, the crowd had closed in to fill the boardwalk.

Randall stood in the doorway, glaring at the sea of stern-jawed faces until enough people moved aside to clear a path, but when Glenn edged outside to follow him, the people instantly milled in. Hands clasped for him.

'Why you leaving with that man?' someone demanded, his comment instantly echoed by dozens of others.

'Because I'm—' Randall said but Glenn didn't hear the rest of his answer as a hubbub of grunted demands went up from people who were spoiling for a fight and didn't want to be placated by a reasonable answer.

Glenn struggled his way clear of the commotion but managed only a single pace towards the road before at least five people pressed in around him, seized his arms, and held him firm. He shot a glance at Randall, who grabbed his hand and tugged and, with Glenn splaying his elbows into stomachs and stamping on feet, they combined forces to drag him clear.

But when they reached the road and turned to Randall's horse, a solid wall of men was standing four deep around it. Each man stood with his arms folded and sported a surly glare that said Randall and Glenn would have to fight every last one of them before they could reach that horse.

Randall rolled his shoulders, as he prepared to start that attempt, but Glenn pointed down the road.

'Reckon as we should get ourselves a drink before we leave town.'

Randall sneered at his suggestion, but on seeing Glenn's raised eyebrows, he glared one last time at the men, then joined him. At a steady and seemingly unconcerned pace, they turned and headed across the road towards the saloon, the crowd outside the sheriff's office peeling away to follow them.

'That mean you know how we can get out of town alive?' Randall asked from the corner of his mouth.

Glenn looked around, seeing the gaggle of people now spreading out as they followed them across the road, but they all kept at least ten yards away.

'Nope. But trying to mount that horse was going to start a fight early.'

Randall followed Glenn's gaze to look up and down the road.

'As opposed to giving us another two minutes before they attack, you mean?'

'Whatever they may think of me, these townsfolk are still decent people. They'll need an excuse to start a fight. So I reckon we don't give them one and they might not attack.'

Randall nodded ahead to the saloon they were approaching.

'And so we just walk in there, buy a drink, then leave, do we?'

'That's the hope.'

Randall snorted. 'Hope is all it is.'

Glenn speeded the pace of his walking. 'Then what's your idea?'

'I reckon we need to find help. Does your sister still live here?'

'She went East after the trial, I reckon.'

'Then have you got *any* friends in Black Rock?'

Glenn glanced left and right to run his gaze across the mass of angry faces. Several people were hurrying on ahead to the saloon, but these men had the eager grins of people who were enjoying the developing situation rather than people who would force a confrontation. Unfortunately, the surly men who had stood around Randall's horse were keeping abreast of them and muttering to each other, goading each other on to be the first to start a confrontation.

'Nope,' Glenn said with firm finality.

'Then people who don't hate you?'

Glenn watched a man bend to pick up a stone then heft it in his right hand.

'Nope.'

'Then what do you suggest?'

Glenn turned on the spot while still walking towards the saloon. He saw people closing in from all directions and judged that the moment when their anger reached a critical mass and they surged in was only moments away.

'I reckon the saloon ain't such a good idea, after all. We got to run.'

'Where to?'

Glenn looked around, searching for a gap in the

mob or a friendly face. He saw neither, but his roving gaze ran across the buildings, passing Bill's mercantile and the courthouse, and alighted on the hotel.

'Archer's hotel,' he murmured, reading the sign above the door.

Randall glanced at the hotel. 'Will that be safe?'

'Don't know, but everybody reckons I killed a Price, and if what Doc Brown said is true and the Archer family hate the Prices, they might be allies. Or at least they might not kill me on sight.'

Randall nodded. 'And that's about the best we can hope for. On the count of three, run for the hotel. One . . .'

The man who was hefting the stone threw back his arm and launched it at Glenn, who ducked, the stone whistling over his head. But when he came up, he didn't wait for Randall to finish his count and ran for the hotel.

And around them, as if the thrown stone was the cue everyone had been waiting for, the mob surged in.

CHAPTER 6

Randall drew alongside Glenn as they sprinted across the road. Around them, the mob poured in from all directions as they charged on to the boardwalk, pounded across it and into the hotel.

The desk clerk, Quincy Gallagher, looked up and peered around the two men, watching Randall slam the door shut. As Randall trapped one man's arm in the door, he hurried out from behind the desk. He helped Randall to prise the arm out, then closed the door, but even with their backs pressed to the door, Glenn judged that it'd be mere seconds before the mob combined forces to barge their way in.

Quincy voiced this view too, and ordered Glenn to help Randall keep the door shut. Then he grabbed a beam that lay on hooks set into the wall and slotted it through heavy hoops on the door behind Randall.

In a co-ordinated move Randall and Glenn stepped forward and the door burst inwards to rattle to a halt against the beam. Glenn judged that it should hold, but with the ready access of the window, and perhaps other doors, he reckoned that if the mob were serious about getting him, this barrier would slow them by only minutes.

'I guess this ain't the first time this has happened?' he asked, pointing at the beam.

Quincy shrugged. 'Nope, but then again, you haven't been in town for a while.'

Then he hurried off, calling out for Niles and Hop to help him.

Glenn confirmed to Randall that these men were the Archer brothers as they backed away across the reception room. The door was still rattling and through the window he could see people milling on the boardwalk, but from their subdued chatter he judged that at the moment their anger wasn't great enough for them to burst in.

Two men hurried in from a back room. They gave the barest glance at Randall and Glenn, then went to the window where they engaged in brief conversation. Glenn recognized the taller of the men as being Niles, the elder, and, if his attitude of fifteen years ago still held, most responsible brother. Hop, probably because Niles was in line to inherit the family business, had always looked for trouble. And sure enough, it was Niles who turned to him and gave a warm smile.

'Glenn Price,' he said, 'it hasn't really changed for you in Black Rock, has it?'

'I guess it hasn't,' Glenn said with a rueful smile, 'but I didn't want to come back here.'

'This got something to do with Myron Cole's death?'

Glenn nodded and without further comment Niles signified that they should follow him into the back room. Glenn noted that Niles was the first person he'd met since leaving jail who hadn't instantly accused him. And something in his placid gaze suggested he bore no malice towards him, and perhaps even thought him innocent.

Hop hung back to instruct Quincy to inform them if the situation outside worsened. As they entered the back room Glenn glanced through the window, noting that although the crowd had thickened, the noise-level was remaining constant.

A solitary lamp and a fire lit the windowless and oppressively stuffy back room. Before the fire sat the huddled husk of a man, whom Glenn didn't recognize immediately until he accepted that he must be Stewart Archer, the man who, with Adam Price, had founded Black Rock. But when he'd last seen him he had been a vital man, who was seemingly invincible and unbowed by the passage of time. Now he was a wizened shell hiding under a blanket that didn't disguise his gaunt frame and bony limbs. And the drooping and drooling face stayed facing the fire and didn't even look up to acknowledge them.

'Randall,' Hop said, joining them, 'we ain't getting involved with this Price. We run a hotel, nothing more.'

'You've done more than enough already,' Randall said as Niles shot Hop an admonishing glance. 'I'll just stay here a while, if you don't mind, and enjoy your hotel's hospitality until the crowd calms. Then I'll leave.'

Niles looked down at Stewart. Although the old man didn't respond in any way that Glenn noticed, Niles nodded and opened his mouth to speak, but

Glenn spoke up first.

'You may hate the Prices,' he said. 'But know this – I ain't one of them.'

Niles just shrugged. Hop snorted.

'You're a Price,' Hop muttered with an assured shake of his fist and a sneer that spoke of an irrational hatred no amount of reasonable talk would placate. 'And before long, we'll run all the Prices out—'

'Hop,' Niles said, 'that ain't the way Pa raised us. We got a hotel to run and that life suits us just fine. We got no desire to run this town.'

Both men looked at Stewart, but still the old man didn't respond.

'It suits *you* just fine,' Hop murmured, turning away to avoid looking at his brother. But Glenn saw the gleam in Hop's eye that said their father would-n't be alive for long, and then he'd resolve his griev-ances his way.

'It does.' Niles turned to Glenn and flashed a smile. 'And we will provide hospitality and a place to sleep, as we would to anyone who needs it, but nothing more.'

Glenn blew out his cheeks as Randall shot him a warning glance, which urged him to consider that they had allies here and not to threaten that hospi-tality by demanding more help than Niles was prepared to give. But Glenn reckoned he'd never get out of Black Rock alive unless he got effective help from someone. And as these people were the only likely candidates, he paced across the room to stand in front of Stewart and stated his case.

'Your family's got problems with the Prices,' he said, speaking loudly in case the infirm old man was hard of hearing, 'but no matter what Hop says, I'm only a Price by name, not blood.'

Stewart didn't look up as Hop snorted and paced across the room to stand by the door, continuing to mutter under his breath about his distrust of the Prices.

Niles watched Hop, then shook his head and joined Glenn. He knelt before Stewart, raised his hand and placed it on his own, then squeezed it.

'What do you reckon, Father?' he asked, his voice soft and encouraging.

Long moments passed in which Glenn became aware of a clock ticking somewhere and of the low hubbub from the crowd outside. Sweat pooled on his skin in the hot room, but before him the old man was shaking, perhaps shivering. Then a rattling wheeze filled the room.

'It has started again,' an aged voice croaked, and for a moment Glenn couldn't believe that this weak voice had come from Stewart. Then the old man raised his head, his neck's lizardlike skin glistening and sallow in the flickering firelight. He fixed him with his rheumy gaze and when he spoke again, his voice was still faint and croaking but this time contained an authoritative hint of the man he had once been. 'The Prices will do anything, double-cross anyone, kill anyone, to find it.'

'Find what?' Glenn said, kneeling beside Niles.

Stewart rolled his rheumy gaze down to consider Glenn.

'The golden spike.' Stewart waved a bony hand and Niles stood. With no discernible effort on his part, he moved Stewart's chair closer to the fire.

Glenn shuffled out of the way and joined Stewart in kneeling beside the fire.

'What's that?' Randall asked.

Stewart stared into the flames for a while before he spoke.

'When the railroad came,' he said, his eyes glazing as he recalled past events, 'Adam and I had a spike struck for the mayor's office as an emblem of why this town was prospering.'

'But someone stole it?' Randall asked, pacing across the room to stand on the other side of Stewart's chair.

Stewart slowly creaked his head round to look up at Randall.

'They did. We never found out who. Adam reckoned it was his no-good drunken brother.' Stewart glanced at Glenn. 'Your father.'

Glenn's mouth fell open and a minute passed before he could control his raging thoughts sufficiently to talk.

'I remember when the spike went missing – the whole town searched for it and had a fair old time too, tearing the place apart. I heard rumours, but I never heard that anyone thought my father stole it.'

'Not everything that gets talked about behind closed doors comes out into the open.'

Glenn gulped, then stood and loomed over the old man. Hop hurried across the room to stand in his way in case he attacked him, but Glenn turned on his heel and paced back to the fire, slapping his fist into his palm.

'My father was poor but he was proud and he'd never steal. When he died I was trying to squeeze out an extra few dollars from the cabinet he'd made. If he'd stolen gold, he wouldn't . . .' Glenn swung round to face Stewart as the full implications of what he'd been told hit him. 'But are you saying somebody reckoned my father stole the spike and killed him while searching for it? And that people in Black Rock knew that, but didn't speak up for me and let me rot in jail?'

From under the blanket, Stewart levered out then waved a bony and admonishing finger at him.

'Suspicions aren't fact.'

'But what *is* fact, Glenn,' Randall said, 'is that Adam did speak up for you and his intervention got you a sentence instead of the rope.'

'And we both know,' Glenn muttered, 'that his intervention came from his conscience speaking. He knew I didn't kill him. He knew whoever did it was looking for the spike, but to say that would admit that he suspected his brother stole it in the first place.'

The room remained silent until Stewart spoke.

'And that is the way of the Prices. Their pride triumphed over sense, as it always has.'

Glenn was in no mood for being placated and he fixed Stewart with his gaze and grunted out his accusation.

'*You* could have spoken up.'

Both Hop and Niles drew in their breaths sharply and Hop moved a pace towards him, but Stewart didn't react.

'And accuse a man who was then my friend and with whom I founded this town?' Stewart considered

64

Glenn until he lowered his gaze, then ejaculated a fluid and rattling snort. 'But then again, you're right and if it helps, I'm sorry I said nothing. At the time it didn't appear important, but now . . .'

'But now I've wasted fifteen years of my life festering away in a stinking—'

'But now,' Randall said, interrupting Glenn, presumably before he could say something that would lose them their only allies and their sanctuary in Black Rock, 'you can't worry about the past. Today, it sounds as if someone is again looking for that spike, and killing to get it.'

'They are,' Stewart said. He fiddled with his blanket, but it slipped and he signalled that Niles should pull it up to his chest. 'But I'll make it simpler for you. Find Arnold Jameson.'

'Why?' Randall snapped.

'Because fifteen years ago Adam hired him to find the spike. He only hired him for a month and he failed, but Arnold had an obsessed look in his eyes that said he'd tear the world apart until he found it.' Stewart shooed Niles away as he continued to fuss with the blanket. 'And if Arnold is still sniffing around, he's close, and Myron Cole won't be the only person he'll kill to get it.'

'We don't know for sure Arnold did kill . . .' Randall said before a flash of pain contorted Stewart's face and his head slumped down on to his chest. Stewart waved feebly towards Niles, who patted his arm, then moved away, mouthing that this discussion had ended and that they should follow him out.

'Who do you suspect stole the spike?' Glenn asked,

ignoring the request.

Niles shot him a harsh glare that said he wouldn't accept him asking his father any more questions.

Glenn continued to glare at Stewart despite the distress in the old man's eyes and the pain that again contorted his features. He hated having to force him to speak, but he needed a solid clue as to who had killed his father, and this man was perhaps the only man who could provide it. But Stewart didn't look at him as he gestured feebly towards the door, his mouth opening and closing.

Glenn looked up to see that Randall and Hop were both staring at him, the contempt in their eyes encouraging him to desist, and so he relented and followed Niles out.

Back in the reception room, a maid joined Niles and he whispered instructions to her to tend to his father. As she hurried into the back room Glenn looked through the window.

Outside, the crowd was still milling with the same intensity and animation as before, but they were showing no sign that they were ready to storm the hotel. On the other hand Glenn also reckoned that there were more people than before, and he didn't detect any sign they would disperse.

Although Niles followed the maid into the back room, Hop stayed to loiter in the reception room. Presently, he shuffled closer.

'What I've just heard changes nothing,' he said, his eyes downcast and not meeting Glenn's. 'I don't want nothing to do with you.'

'Then I guess I got no choice but to accept that.'

Hop nodded and looked up, this time meeting Glenn's eye. He gestured outside.

'But I guess that crowd won't stay outside for ever. Someone is going to act before too much longer. I'll see about getting you a spare horse out back.' He shrugged. 'And perhaps a change of clothes.'

'Obliged,' Glenn said.

'Don't be. I just want to get rid of you.' Hop pointed up the stairs. 'Now stay out of the way and don't let anyone see you.'

Glenn nodded. With Randall at his side he headed up the stairs. The first-floor balcony doubled back over the reception room with rooms coming off on either side. At the front was a window that let him see down into the road.

Randall and Glenn stood on either side of the window, staying far enough back for none of the mob to be able to see them. And looking outside, Glenn's concerns grew in proportion to the expanding size of the crowd, which he could now see had doubled in the time since they'd sought sanctuary in here.

Everyone was chatting and they appeared more eager to share news of what had happened than to display their anger. Glenn still judged that they needed provocation before acting.

But as more people continued to swell the crowd, the chances of that happening grew.

'You reckon you can find Arnold?' Glenn asked.

Randall shrugged. 'Like I told you, I got no interest in this no more. This is too complicated for me.'

'But you must want to work out what's happening?'

'I'm no lawman and I got no personal interest in this. And the chances of a bounty are getting smaller as that crowd gets larger. As soon as this mob calms down, I'm leaving.'

Glenn craned his neck as he peered up and down the road.

'Then you'd better hope they don't goad themselves into lynching us.'

Randall pulled Glenn back from the window.

'And you staying out of sight will help that.'

Glenn shook his head. He pulled away from Randall and drew his attention to a bustle of people who were heading away from the main group outside the hotel. He watched them with interest until they stopped outside the sheriff's office, their gesturing to each other conveying they were debating what had happened to the sheriff.

'You believe everything that Stewart said?' Glenn asked as one man hammered on the office door.

'Some of it might be true, and maybe it does explain why your father was murdered.'

Glenn sighed and pulled away from the window to look at Randall.

'I've spent years hating you for catching me and even more time hating the people who put me away, but until now, I hadn't realized how good it is to hear that you reckon I'm innocent.'

'I didn't say that. I bear no feelings towards you either good or bad.' Randall sighed. 'But if all the facts had come out, I'd have still brought you in. But I reckon they shouldn't have found you guilty.'

'That helps.' Glenn pointed outside. 'But I need

more than just you who reckon I'm innocent now.'

Randall followed the direction of Glenn's pointing and winced.

The office door was swinging open to reveal a groggy Sheriff Price. Two men were helping to move him, but he pushed these people aside, swayed before regaining his footing, then barged away the people gathered outside his door, to stand on the edge of the boardwalk. He felt his jaw while listening to a man explain what had happened. He nodded, his gaze rising until it rested on the mob outside the hotel.

Then he set his hat forward and headed across the road, trailing people behind him. The mob ahead parted, then closed behind him like a stick drawn through water.

Inside, footfalls pounded up the stairs. Then Niles hurtled down the corridor, his eyes wide.

'We got trouble,' he shouted, sliding to a halt.

'We've seen,' Glenn said. 'Emerson Price is heading here. Has Hop got that horse ready?'

'He hasn't had the time yet.'

'Then are you prepared to defend us, or are you letting the mob in?'

'Like I said, we stay out of trouble and don't take sides.' Niles edged from foot to foot then shrugged. 'But either way, no Price is setting foot on Archer property without a proper invite.'

Glenn patted Niles's back. With Niles leading the way and with Randall following behind, he headed down the corridor to the top of the stairs. In the reception room below Hop and Quincy were standing before the door with guns drawn. Hop shouted a threat through the door, but the rising clamour from outside drowned out his words.

Then a pounding started on the door, as of another beam hammering against it. The beam holding the door in place rattled and creaked, but the heavy hoops holding it in place stayed firm and wouldn't let the door open.

Then a huge crack sounded and the entire door and frame rocked forward. It crashed to the floor and from Glenn's foreshortened view of the room below, he saw a block of people spill inside. At their front was Sheriff Price.

Hop and Quincy backed away as Emerson advanced on them and Glenn saw the lawman's legs, then body heave into view as he paced towards the stairs, a solid phalanx of shouting and arm-waving people following him into the hotel.

'Put those guns down,' Emerson ordered, 'or join that excuse for a Price on the end of a rope.'

Quincy instantly lowered his gun, Hop reluctantly followed him.

At the top of the stairs Niles grabbed Glenn's arm and pulled him out of view and down the corridor, cutting off his view of what Sheriff Price did next. He heard Hop complain about the intrusion and damage, but the explosion of responses from the crowd left him in no doubt that the mob was in no mood to listen to reason.

Niles led them into the first room along the corridor. Once inside Glenn hurried to the window to look outside. He saw the crowd below, which was now about ten deep. Every person was shoving forward as they all tried to follow Emerson into the hotel. But from their slow pace, Glenn judged that only a few of them would get in. And sure enough, presently the backmost members stopped shoving, accepting they wouldn't be able to reach the hotel and instead craned their necks in eagerness to see what was happening ahead.

Randall joined him at the window.

'This ain't looking good,' he said.

'Yeah.' Glenn pointed across the road. 'But they haven't moved your horse. If enough of them get inside, we might be able to get out through the window and make a run for it.'

Randall gave a sceptical nod, then drew Glenn back from the window to avoid anyone seeing him.

'Running didn't help you last time,' he said.

'Yeah,' Niles said from beside the door. 'Give Hop a chance. He may not like you, but he hates the other Prices more and he can be persuasive when he wants to be. And if all else fails, Pa still commands a kind of authority that even Emerson's star can't provide.'

Glenn blew out his cheeks. 'That mob didn't look as if it wanted to listen to persuasion.'

'I guess you're right there, but there ain't been a lynching in Black Rock since . . . since the last time they tried to lynch you. If anyone can talk them down, they can.'

Glenn glanced at Randall, who returned a sorry shake of the head that didn't hold out any hope that a frail old man and his argumentative son, armed with just words, could hold back a hundred angry people.

CHAPTER 7

Glenn, Randall and Niles stood around the door, listening to the clatter of the rising rumpus in the reception room below. Glenn could hear Hop's voice but not his words, but he could heard Sheriff Price's retorts and they were all demands that he hand over Glenn or face the consequences.

'I guess it doesn't pay to get on the wrong side of the Prices,' Glenn said to no one in particular. He listened to a thud from downstairs, then to scuffling, as if a fight had broken out on the stairs. He spoke rapidly to Niles, more to still his growing fear than to try to glean information. 'If Arnold is searching for the golden spike, who will he go after next?'

'Not many are left for him to go after. Most of those who were involved fifteen years ago are dead.' Niles counted on his fingers, mouthing names. 'Judge Mitchell is still working and, aside from Matlock Langhorne, there's probably nobody left who had a direct link with what happened fifteen years ago.'

'And where is he?'

'Matlock is our most celebrated citizen,' Niles said

with bemusement in his tone as he flinched back.

Glenn shrugged. 'I ain't been keeping up with events here for the last fifteen years.'

'I guess not. He went east and now he's a state senator.'

'And nobody else is alive?'

'There's your sister. She went east too.'

Glenn had always assumed Katie would go in search of her real family, and he made a silent vow that if he survived the next few hours, he would seek her out. Glenn also caught something odd in Niles's tone, as if he was trying to tell him something in that simple comment. If he hadn't have heard numerous feet pounding up the stairs, he'd have questioned him more.

Niles signified that they should join him in pressing themselves against the wall. Then along with Randall he drew his gun, as doors further down the corridor slammed open, the sounds getting closer.

Then their door burst open.

Glenn flinched back, unprepared for the solid wall of humanity that surged through the door and closed around him. Randall loosed off a high warning blast into the ceiling, which failed to slow the mob. Within moments people surrounded him and prised the gun from his fingers.

Hands clawed at Glenn. Then the press of people bodily lifted him from the floor, marched him to the door and into the corridor. He tried to meet someone's eye but all he could see was staring eyes infused with bloodlust and wide-open mouths shouting out their anger. He recognized several people, but none of them met his gaze, and the people who couldn't have known him from fifteen years ago were just as angry.

Through the press of people he caught glimpses of Randall, who was faring as badly as he was. He saw him disappear under a tangle of people. His right arm clawed its way out, but then disappeared again.

To his side, Niles had been pinned against the corridor wall and disarmed.

At the top of the stairs, the mob stopped dragging him on, but only because so many people were blocking the stairs they couldn't manoeuvre him down them.

Then a gunshot blasted, slicing through the clamour and bringing about a sudden reduction in the noise level. In the silence, a space opened up in the centre of the reception room below him.

In the centre of this space stood Sheriff Emerson Price with his gun thrust high. He fired again for emphasis, this time the sound echoed in the silence. He paraded around on the spot, ensuring he had everyone's attention.

To Glenn's side, the crowd manoeuvred Niles until he stood side by side with Glenn, with Randall held behind them. Each man had at least three men holding him from behind.

'Now that we have Glenn Price,' Emerson shouted as he looked around, meeting several people's enthusiastic gazes, 'what do we do with him?'

'Lynch him,' the cry went up, the sound echoing and gaining momentum. 'Lynch him, lynch him, lynch him!'

A rope appeared. Eager hands were raised to carry it over the tops of people's heads. Then a length rose up to snake over an exposed beam and was pulled taut.

Glenn struggled, but found no give in everyone's firm grips. He looked around the mass of suffused and firm-jawed faces, searching for a friendly look, but could find only Quincy, and he was also being held.

Hop and Stewart were in the doorway to the back room. Hop was straining to see what was happening while protecting his seated father from the crush of the crowd. Then his gaze locked on to Glenn's eyes. He gave a pained shrug, perhaps signifying that despite his distrust of him he wanted to help, but could do nothing against so many.

Glenn returned a nod, then thrust himself forward, not to seek his freedom but to let Hop see that his brother was also being held.

Hop paled. He bent to speak to Stewart, then barged people aside until he reached the clear space beside Sheriff Price. By now the rope was dangling and one man was standing on another man's shoulders to shorten it to a length that would let a man dangle with his neck unbroken and so die in the slowest possible way.

Hop nudged past these men and stood before Sheriff Price.

'Wait!' he shouted. He turned on the spot, waving his arms above his head.

'We've waited fifteen years for justice,' Emerson said, sneering at him. 'We ain't waiting another minute.'

Emerson looked around with his hands held aloft,

seeking confirmation, and the crowd returned a baying cry that they wanted to see Glenn swing.

'And what has my brother done to deserve this?'

'Your . . .' Emerson nodded with sudden understanding. 'I'm just holding him for now. Don't worry. I'll release him when this is over. But Glenn Price gets justice here, today.'

Sheriff Price and Hop locked gazes and an unspoken argument flared in the eyes of both men. At the top of the stairs, Glenn could only guess about its nature, but reckoned it probably confirmed that Stewart's hatred of Adam had passed on to the next generation of Archers and Prices. But whereas Adam's death ensured that Emerson no longer felt a need to stop that hatred boiling over into revenge, Hop was still shackled.

And sure enough it was Hop who was first to lower his head. Uncomplaining, he let two men lead him back to his father, leaving Emerson to gesture to the men holding Glenn. Then Glenn was bustled down the stairs, but the people holding him stopped after negotiating three steps and looked down into the hallway. Over the heads of the people below, Glenn saw that a new man had entered the hotel.

Glenn narrowed his eyes and confirmed that this man was Clyde Price, Emerson's brother and the prospective mayor of Black Rock. Despite Glenn's doubt that this man would help him, Clyde looked up at the noose, frowned, then forced his way into the hotel to stand before Emerson.

'What are you doing?' he demanded.

'I'm dealing with our problem,' Emerson said, not

meeting his brother's eye.

'By lynching . . .' Clyde looked up the stairs and considered Glenn. 'By lynching . . . Glenn Price?'

Emerson turned to look at Clyde and their gazes locked. Observing both men's raised eyebrows and firm jaws, Glenn reckoned that they were silently debating a subject of which they couldn't speak aloud.

'We have to,' Emerson murmured eventually. 'You know that.'

'We have to do nothing. We will abide by the rule of law in Black Rock and try Glenn the proper way tomorrow – as we agreed we'd do . . . tomorrow. We will do it *tomorrow*.'

Glenn noticed Clyde's repeated emphasis of the word 'tomorrow' and although he didn't understand what that meant, right now his only interest was in whether it would earn him a temporary reprieve.

'Why wait until then?' Emerson said, placing his hands on his hips. 'Everything is in place. His death changes nothing. It's just one less thing to worry about.'

Clyde looked up and considered Glenn, his eyes blank, extinguishing Glenn's faint hope that Clyde's complaints came from a desire for proper justice.

'I guess you're right,' he said and turned away. 'Then stop wasting time and do what you must. Hang him.'

A huge cheer echoed. Then everyone bustled. Glenn saw Hop fight his way to the bottom of the stairs, presumably to talk to Niles when he passed by him, and several men got to work on ensuring the noose was secure. The people on the stairs filed down into the clear space in the reception room to give everyone further up the stairs sufficient space to escort Glenn and the others downstairs. And when a gap opened up, they pushed Niles forwards to join Glenn.

Niles resisted for long enough to halt his progress and shoot Glenn a hopeless and regret-filled glance. Glenn could do nothing but look back at him. Then the mob dragged Niles down into the reception room.

The three men holding Glenn pushed him forward to head down the stairs towards the waiting noose, but with the available space still being limited, they got in each others' way. One of the pair of hands holding him released his arms. And in desperation, Glenn seized one last chance to gain his freedom.

He went limp, dragging the other two men forward, then threw back his arms.

He tore himself away from the first pair of hands and dropped to his knees. He picked up the last man holding him and threw him over his shoulders and down the stairs. The man landed on the backs of the people below and tumbled a swath of men to their knees at the foot of the stairs.

In the temporary confusion, Glenn turned and fought his way through the mass of people at the top of the stairs, aiming to reach the clear corridor beyond.

He slugged one man's jaw, headbutted another, and kicked and stamped and flailed his arms, using every ounce of the berserk energy he'd wound up inside since he'd seen the rope.

He saw Randall struggle and gain his freedom for long enough to trip one man up and slug another man's jaw, but then others pressed around him and pinned him to the wall. But with the crowd's attention split between them, Glenn found himself with just two men between him and the corridor beyond.

He thrust his head down and bundled into the first man, lifted him off the floor and threw him over a shoulder. Then he charged the last man. That man scrambled for his gun, but Glenn slammed both hands together and slapped them into his face, wheeling him over the balustrade. The man threw out an arm to hold on and dangle before falling into the crowd below.

Then Glenn ran for freedom. His guts rumbled with a hopeless acceptance of the fact he was only avoiding his inevitable demise for perhaps a few seconds, but he still had to try or face a certain lynching.

He hurtled down the corridor, zigzagging from one side to the other and hurling pictures and mirrors from the wall. He stopped to topple a sideboard as he sought to slow down his pursuers.

At the end of the corridor, another corridor led off to the left and he glanced to one side as he skirted around the corner. A sprawling straggle of men were chasing after him and leaping over the furniture he'd strewn in his wake. And they were just yards behind him.

Then he looked straight ahead down the corridor, and saw there were three rooms on either side.

But the corridor itself was a dead end.

CHAPTER 8

With his pursuers stomping closer to the corner of the corridor, Glenn grabbed the only piece of furniture along the hall, a large cabinet. He tried to topple it, but it was too heavy and he wasted valuable seconds as he failed to knock it over.

By the time he gave up, men were hurrying round the corridor after him.

He broke into a run, the pursuers just feet behind him. He ran past one door, two, then had no choice but to throw open the last door on the left.

He faced a room that was similar to the one he'd hidden in before – with a bed, a sideboard, a window. He swirled round to slam the door shut, but one man, then a second, pushed into it and knocked him backwards.

He righted himself and threw a punch at the first man. That man ducked it and returned a short uppercut to the chin, which wheeled Glenn back on to the bed.

He put out a hand to stop himself falling, then righted himself, but already another three men had bustled into the room. Glenn turned. Their hands scraped his back but failed to grab hold of him. He vaulted the bed and ran for the window. He threw it open, noting there was a balcony and beneath that the main road where the crowd was milling.

A hand grabbed his waist, but he kicked out, freed himself and tumbled out on to the balcony. He slammed the window shut behind him, forcing the nearest pursuer to snatch his hands back to avoid having them crushed.

Then he turned to discover whether he stood any chance of finding freedom outside. He saw none.

Below him, heads craned up from the fifty or so people in the road and a forest of arms pointed up at him. Then everyone bayed into the hotel with a cacophony of righteous anger that he was here.

Glenn looked around, noticing that Randall's horse was still outside the sheriff's office, but with the people around the hotel being at least five deep, it might as well have been 1,000 miles away.

He looked up. The false-fronted hotel was two storeys high and if he could climb around fifteen feet he could slip over that front and gain the roof. But he saw no handholds in the smooth wood. He stood back, searching for a potential route for him to climb, but then the window creaked open.

He stood back, darting his gaze around with ever more frantic efforts until he noted the only possible way of prolonging his temporary freedom – the balcony to the room on the other side of the corridor. It was around ten feet away and identical to the balcony on which he stood.

He swirled round, leapt on to the balustrade, wheeling his arms as he righted himself. Then he hurled himself across the gap. His chest hammered into the wooden rail as he folded over it. He hung on, his feet searching for purchase, then he tried to loop an elbow on to the top rail, but he missed and slipped.

His legs dropped until he dangled at full stretch. Below him, his swaying feet were out of everyone's reach, but people jumped up and tried to grab them. Cries went up for someone to climb on top of another man's shoulders and grab him.

Glenn whirled his legs, trying to catch hold of the bottom of the balcony with his knee and drag himself up. Then another man jumped from the adjoining balcony and slammed into the railings beside him. That man clung on as Glenn did, but he didn't have as firm a grip as Glenn had and he slipped.

He tumbled towards the waiting arms of the crowd below but, with a trailing hand, he lunged for and grabbed Glenn's right leg, then held on.

With this man's weight dragging on him, Glenn felt as if he was tearing his arms from their sockets.

His hands slipped as the man's weight pulled him taut. He kicked out, but the man still held on. He raised his left leg and stamped down on the man's face and this time the man tumbled on to the backs of the waiting crowd.

The man knocked a circle of people over and Glenn considered jumping down, using their confusion to run for the horse, but everyone quickly gained their feet.

Then he saw several men draw guns.

In manic desperation, Glenn looped an arm over the balustrade and tugged himself up. A gunshot sounded, the slug tore splinters from the railing, inches from Glenn's left hand. Glenn redoubled his scrambling efforts as he hurled himself over the balustrade and on to the balcony.

He looked up. As this was the last room on this side of the hotel there were projections on the side of the false front up which he could climb to reach the roof. He crawled to the side of the balcony and reached for the nearest, but a volley of gunfire ripped into the wall before his outstretched hand. He darted back, deciding that attempting the exposed climb would just get him a bullet in the back.

With no chance of freedom from heading down to the road or up on to the roof, Glenn threw open the window and rolled through. Outside, a chorus of shouting went up from the crowd to the people looking out of the next window, telling what he'd done. Those messages were relayed into the room, then to the corridor.

By the time he reached the door, he heard scrambling footfalls in the corridor as a burst of people hurried towards it.

He grabbed the cabinet beside the door and dragged it across the doorway. The door hurled open but slammed into the back of the cabinet, rocking it forward, but Glenn continued dragging until it fully blocked the doorway.

It was heavy enough to delay anyone trying to

open the door just by pounding on it and already the people in the corridor were shouting to others to get at him through the window.

Glenn hurried to the window, all the time looking for something with which to barricade himself in and win himself a few more minutes of relative freedom and perhaps a hope that another method of escape might occur to him.

But he saw no furniture that was large enough, except the bed.

So he grabbed the bed, hoisted it on to its side, then dragged it to the window. As he closed off the view from outside, he saw one man already leaping on to the balcony.

He swirled round. In the darkened room he saw that the door was open to the utmost that could be managed, which was only a foot, but somebody had wedged a plank into the gap and was now widening that gap.

He looked around the rest of the room, but with the light level having dropped, he saw something he'd missed on his first glance.

There was a second window. It was small and on the side wall, and Glenn hurried over to it and looked out, then down.

His heart leapt with renewed hope.

Down below was the alley between the hotel and the courthouse and, in the short length of it that he could see, nobody was loitering.

He levered the window open and peered around. Still he saw nobody below.

The drop was around twenty feet, high enough to

twist an ankle if he didn't land properly. So Glenn dashed back to the bed, dragged off a blanket, and looped it around the table beside the window. Then he swirled the blanket round into a makeshift rope and hurled an end through the window.

As the blanket rolled down to stop fifteen feet from the ground, he jumped on to the window ledge. Then he grabbed the blanket and braced his feet against the wall.

He took one last look into the room and saw the cabinet shake as the mob slowly prised open the door. The bed was teetering and was almost ready to be toppled.

He looked down. The alley was still deserted and if he gained it before anyone in the road noticed him he would buy himself enough time to run. But he didn't know the current layout of the town and he didn't know where he could run to or where he could hide. His freedom would last for at best another few minutes.

Then a wild idea came to him.

The cabinet by the door was identical to the kind his father had once made and he guessed that maybe the Archer family had bought it from him. When Glenn had been a child, he had often hidden in cabinets such as this one in games with his sister.

And perhaps he could do that again.

He swung himself back on to the window ledge and into the room. He checked that the blanket was still dangling as if it were a rope, then he hurried across the room to the cabinet.

He'd grown since he'd last tried to squeeze into

such a confined space, but when he threw open the door, only spare blankets were inside. He crammed his body into the space and closed the door.

From the corridor he heard shouting. Through the crack between the door and the frame he saw the bed topple over and a line of men clamber in through the window.

But their gazes fell on the other open window at the side of the room. Then the cabinet shook as the people in the corridor levered open the door wide enough for more men to surge into the room.

'He's got away,' someone shouted.

'He's headed into the alley,' another shouted down through the main window. 'Cut him off! Cut him off!'

Then they spilled out of the room, shouting out to the people in the corridor as to where he'd gone, that cry echoing on until it reached the people outside the hotel.

Glenn crunched down in his confined space, feeling the first twinges of cramp attack him but still being relieved and amazed that his ruse appeared to have worked. He saw the remaining people file out through the room and none of them gave even a second glance at the cabinet.

Two men did stay at the window to shout encouragement to the people below as they hurried down the alley. Glenn smiled when he heard someone shout back that he'd seen their quarry heading around the back of the courthouse.

Presently the men at the window gave up shouting advice and hurried off to join in the more enjoyable activity of the manhunt.

Then he was alone.

He was still trapped in a town where everyone but a few people wanted to lynch him, but he had earned himself a respite. And he'd earned himself time to think and perhaps even to work out how he could prove himself innocent of the crimes this town was determined to heap upon him.

By degrees silence returned to the hotel, although through the windows he could still hear the excited cries of a town embarking on a manhunt where everyone knew theft quarry had to be close.

Later, chatter restarted in the hotel between Randall, Niles and Hop as they headed down the corridor, righting furniture. Although Glenn couldn't hear everything they said, he judged that Randall was offering consoling comments about Niles's attempts to stop what had happened, although Hop mainly complained about the damage the Prices had done to the hotel.

When they reached the end of the corridor and Niles peered into the room opposite Glenn's, he heard Randall speak.

'Where do you reckon he's gone?' he asked.

'Don't know,' Niles said. 'There's plenty of places to hide even in our small town, but I can't think of anywhere where he can hide for ever.'

'Glenn is a resourceful man. It took me some effort to find him the last time.'

'So where would you look?'

'I got no interest. I'm just a man who brings 'em in for the bounty and nobody's paying for my services here.'

That was all the encouragement Glenn needed that these people were still supporting him, or at least were not against him, and he coughed.

'What was that?' Niles asked.

'*That* was me,' Glenn said. He pushed open the cabinet door and tumbled himself on to the floor. He stretched his cramped limbs, then rolled to his feet to stand in the doorway.

Niles emitted a snorting laugh and even Randall smiled.

'That was sure taking a risk,' Randall said.

'Like Niles said, there ain't many safe hiding-places in town.' Glenn patted Niles on the back. 'And this place is one of the few.'

'It is,' Niles said, 'but not for long. Soon, somebody will work out that you must be hiding in here. We have to get you somewhere safe, and quickly.'

'But where? I ain't exactly got many friends in this town.'

Niles offered some consoling but not particularly helpful platitudes, then went into the room in which Glenn had just hidden and started righting furniture. Hop hurried back down the corridor to get the horse he'd promised earlier. Randall watched him leave, then gave Glenn a quick pat on the back.

'And while you wait for that horse,' he said as he followed Hop, 'I'll bid you goodbye and wish you luck.'

'You're not leaving without me, surely?' Glenn shouted at his receding back.

Randall stopped and rubbed his chin. He glanced back, a rare amused twinkle in his eye suggesting he wasn't seriously considering the request.

'Glenn, it's time you accepted something. I ain't siding with you. I ain't letting anyone think I've sided with you, and I sure as hell ain't risking joining you on the end of a rope.'

'I can't believe you'd walk away from all of this.'

'Don't care what you believe.' Randall tipped his hat. 'I'm getting away while they're searching for you.'

Randall turned, but Glenn hurried on, catching up with Randall at the corner. He grabbed Randall's arm and spun him round.

'I don't reckon you mean that. You helped me back in Emerson's office when you didn't have to and then again back on the stairs. You claim you just bring 'em in for the bounty, but you care about my fate more than you'll admit.'

Randall snorted and looked down at Glenn's hand.

'Nice theory, but I ain't got the time to debate it. I'm leaving, and you'll move that hand before I snap it off.'

Glenn raised his hand and let Randall walk away, but when he reached the top of the stairs, he coughed.

'I don't reckon you're leaving. You're going after Arnold Jameson.'

Randall took one pace down the stairs then stopped and looked at Glenn.

'Why would I do that?'

'Because you got a personal score to settle with him after he got away from you.'

Randall shrugged. 'No bounty, no interest.'

'Except he's on the trail of the golden spike and that sure has to interest you.'

Randall grinned. 'Like I said – no bounty, no interest.'

'Then listen to this – you'll go after him because he has a score to settle with you and you're not the kind of man who sits around waiting for someone to find him.'

Randall waved in a dismissive manner at Glenn and headed off down the stairs.

'If I choose to go after Arnold,' he shouted over his shoulder, 'that's my concern, and it's got nothing to do with you.'

'It has.' Glenn waited until Randall was moving out of his view, then made his offer. 'Because I know where Arnold is hiding out.'

CHAPTER 9

Glenn stood his ground as Randall stormed down the corridor towards him.

'I ain't got time for another one of your ruses,' Randall grunted. 'You may have fooled everyone in town, but you won't fool me.'

'That was no ruse. I *do* know where you'll find Arnold Jameson.'

Randall stopped two paces in front of Glenn and aimed a firm finger at him.

'Glenn, I only just decided not to hand you over to Emerson for the bounty, but this town is mighty worked up and I will change my mind if you waste any more of my time. So tell me what you know, now!'

Glenn raised his chin to avoid gulping and moistened his dry throat.

Anything he said would betray the fact that while he was hiding in the cabinet he'd formed only the vaguest of theories as to where Arnold would be. If he were to voice it, he guessed Randall would either not believe him or hit him for daring to suggest it.

Either way, he wouldn't help him leave town.

So he stared at Randall, watching his face redden by the moment and his hands open and close.

Glenn shook his head. 'I won't do that.'

'Then I'll leave you here to die.' Randall turned and headed away.

'Wait! Take me with you,' Glenn said, but this time Randall reached the stairs and continued down them. Glenn broke into a run. He hurried down the corridor then pounded down the stairs after Randall.

'Quit chasing me,' Randall grunted as he reached the bottom of the stairs.

'Randall,' Glenn murmured, the noose that still dangled from the ceiling catching his eye, 'we *can* work together.'

'I don't have partners.' Randall continued walking towards the wide open doorway, but he stopped before the toppled door and lowered his voice. 'But just tell me what you know. I'll do the rest.'

'Randall, we need each other,' Glenn said, loitering in the shadows at the bottom of the stairs in case anyone happened to go past the door outside and see him through the doorway. 'You got the firepower and the ability to track men down. I got information about this town and its people.'

'You got information that's fifteen years out of date.'

'Only fifteen-year-old information will solve what's happening here.'

Randall straightened then paced into the doorway to look up and down the road. He nodded, then glanced over his shoulder, taking in the noose before he looked at Glenn.

'You know something, Glenn? You're right. But the trouble is, I'm just a man who brings 'em in for the bounty. I don't need your kind of trouble.'

'And without my help that trouble will still follow you.'

Randall looked out into the road.

'I'd start running now if I were you,' he said. 'Somebody will work out where you are before long.'

'And when I run, you'll never find Arnold Jameson. Is that what you want, Randall?'

In the open doorway, Randall looked back at Glenn. He sighed and closed his eyes for a moment.

Ten minutes later Glenn shuffled around inside Hop's clothes. Hop was a bulky man and so the clothes dangled off his lean frame, but although this disguise would fool only casual observers, he reckoned some form of disguise was his best chance of getting out of town. And in case that failed, he reluctantly accepted that the gun he'd borrowed from Hop would have to do the rest.

Randall left the hotel first and collected his horse along with Hop's mount. Glenn watched him through the hotel window, staying in the shadows, and saw that Randall didn't hurry, attempting to convey that he wasn't worried. But then again, he wasn't and it was Glenn who was doing all the worrying.

After what seemed like an age Randall mounted his horse then led the other horse across the road. He pulled up outside the hotel and glanced around, presenting an image of an unconcerned man. Luckily, the people out on the road were still scurrying around on the manhunt and didn't so much as give a second glance to a man who had been held while they tried to lynch Glenn.

Glenn watched from the reception room, urging him to make the signal, but Randall waited until nobody was close or heading past the hotel. Then he gestured.

Glenn took a deep breath and paced out on to the boardwalk, Hop's hat thrust so low he could see only his feet. He mounted the spare horse and, with minimal fuss, turned it and strolled towards the edge of town.

The way ahead was clear and Glenn had to fight back a desire to spur his horse and gallop away, but he accepted that Randall's plan of appearing unconcerned would raise the least suspicion. He even joined Randall in frequently glancing around in a manner that any person who was leaving town might.

But once they'd cleared the last building they broke into a trot and swung round to head towards the rail-tracks.

Randall had followed Arnold's trail to the tracks on the previous night, before he'd lost it. When they reached them, Glenn expected Randall to demand to know what information he claimed to have. But instead, he rode up and down the tracks, apparently determined to use his own tracking skills before resorting to Glenn.

Presently, he grunted to himself and headed off without looking at Glenn, who followed him.

'Found his tracks?' he shouted as he drew along-side.

'Yup.'

'How do you know they're his?'

'I'm a bounty hunter. I know.' Randall turned to face him. 'Want to make your guess as to where you reckon he'll be before I catch up with him?'

'I'll wait until you've lost his trail.' Glenn craned his neck as he looked ahead. 'And that'll be in about five miles.'

Randall snorted his disbelief in Glenn's opinion, but five miles further on they reached the creek about twenty miles downriver from the spot where Glenn had tried to escape yesterday.

The tracks Randall had been following led into the water and despite searching for the next half-hour, Randall couldn't find where they emerged. So he turned to head downriver, still without question-ing Glenn.

'Where you going now?' Glenn asked.

'I know Arnold,' Randall said, not looking at Glenn. 'He'll have headed away from town.'

'And what about me?'

'You can go to hell or crawl into whatever hole you can find.'

'I ain't doing that. I reckon I'll go to see Arnold on my own.' Glenn pointed over his shoulder. 'He went upriver.'

Randall raised the reins, but then lowered them. He took a deep breath and fixed Glenn with his icy gaze.

'This is your last chance, Glenn. I ain't playing no

more games with you. I got you out of town like I promised and if you want to tell me what you know, do it. If you don't want to, don't.' Randall glanced back towards town. 'But after you escaped, I reckon they'll be offering plenty more bounty on your head. You won't survive for long on your own, especially if I choose to go after that bounty.'

'All right. Arnold headed that way,' Glenn said, signifying his assumption of Arnold's movements with a wave of the hand. 'Then he went round the black rock and to . . . to Doc Brown's place.'

Randall raised his eyebrows. 'Interesting thought. Arnold is injured and Alan didn't have enough time to clean up his shoulder or head. So he might need help.'

'It isn't that.' Glenn took a deep breath. 'Doc Brown let him go yesterday.'

Randall flared his eyes. 'Take that back. Alan Brown is my friend.'

'I know, but Arnold could have fooled us easily about how injured he was, but he couldn't have fooled a doctor. Brown must have known Arnold was feigning his injury.'

'Like I said, Alan Brown wouldn't do that.'

'Perhaps he . . .' Glenn glanced away, preferring to keep private the wild assumption that had led him to this theory and instead settling for providing a simpler answer. 'Perhaps Arnold didn't give him no choice.'

'Why?'

'Because aside from Brown there are few people left in town who were involved in the events of fifteen years ago. He confirmed my pa was dead. And if Arnold is finding and killing off anyone who was involved in those events while he searches for the spike, Brown could be next.'

'Then why didn't he kill him yesterday?'

'Because he needs his help, but as soon as Brown's tended to his wounds, he won't need him no more. And the longer we stand here talking, the greater the chance we won't get there before he stops needing him.'

Randall glanced towards Brown's house. He sighed and held his hand to the side, signifying that Glenn should lead.

Glenn returned a grateful nod. They galloped along beside the creek, but when they left it Randall chose a cautious route to Brown's house round the towering black rock that kept them out of sight of anyone looking from the building. They tethered their horses beside the rock, about a quarter-mile from the house. Randall ordered Glenn to stay where he was and headed off to scout around the house from closer to. When he returned he reported in a matter-of-fact manner that Brown had company.

Glenn didn't request any more information, but he guessed from Randall's irritated gaze that Arnold was that company. He also guessed that reminding Randall of his correct assumption wouldn't be well received.

Without further comment they hurried from the rock on foot, then ran on a direct line towards the windowless side of the house.

As they closed on the side of the house, Glenn

noted that four horses were tethered inside the barn. When Arnold had attacked them by the creek yesterday several men had run away; he guessed that these men could still be with him and aiding him.

They reached the house and peered around the side of the building, confirming that nobody was outside. Then, with Randall leading, they crawled along the side of the wall to reach the window to the main room.

Together they edged up to look through the window and into the room where Brown had talked with them yesterday while he examined Arnold. Several people were within. Glenn glanced at each man in turn until he confirmed that Arnold Jameson was there. He was sitting on the table with his back to him. Brown was probing his arm.

They both darted their heads back from the window. Randall stood to the side of the window, drew his gun, and moved towards the front door, but Glenn pulled him back and signified that they should slip in through the next window to the other room.

Randall mouthed a silent question as to why they should do that, but Glenn shook his head and headed there anyhow. He heard Randall utter an irritated grunt, but he still followed him.

Acting as quietly as he could, Glenn levered open the shutters and they slipped in through the window and paced across the room to the door to the main room, where they listened.

Glenn listened for long enough to hear that while Brown was working on Arnold's arm, Arnold was talking with another man, but about nothing of interest. Then he looked around the room.

He wasn't sure what he was looking for, but the hunch he had backed when he'd directed Randall to come here was that yesterday there was something in this room that Brown hadn't wanted him to see.

Quickly, the large cabinet standing against the back wall drew his gaze. It was identical to the one in which he'd hidden back in the hotel room. More important, it was identical to the one his father had made and which Glenn had tried to sell to Matlock Langhorne on that fateful day when his father had been murdered.

And when he stood before it, he saw a scratch down the side that he'd made when it had slipped while he was attempting to move it. He also saw the repaired door that had resulted from the same accident. There was no doubt about it. This was the same piece of furniture that had once been in his home. It was also the cabinet before which he'd found his father's body.

He quietly opened the doors, not to search inside but to give himself time to think while he worked out how this cabinet fitted into everything that was happening. Then he fingered around the sides, finding that the topmost panel had been broken off, then repaired. He fingered around the sides of the panel, searching for the weakest point, then prised the panel away to peer inside.

Randall had stopped listening at the door to watch him. Now he joined Glenn in peering into the hollow he'd uncovered. He raised his eyebrows.

'This cabinet,' Glenn whispered, 'has something to do with why my pa died. And perhaps as to why Myron died too.'

Randall rose on tiptoe to look into the space that Glenn had opened up.

'Because somebody hid the spike in here?'

'That's what I'm thinking, and whoever killed my father was searching for it.' Glenn frowned. 'And Doc Brown didn't want me to see that he now owns this cabinet.'

Randall narrowed his eyes, his voice rising despite the need to be quiet.

'You'd better not be suggesting he had anything to do with no murders.'

'I'm not,' Glenn muttered, urging Randall to quieten with a downward wave of his hands, 'unless you can think of another explanation.'

Randall pursed his lips then stood back to look the cabinet up and down.

'Maybe whoever killed your father was interested in the cabinet for the spike, but Alan wanted it for something else.' Randall opened a drawer and gestured at the sprawl of letters within. 'Like letters, or . . .'

Glenn considered Randall's unconvincing answer, but he didn't want to risk annoying him any more while Arnold was close enough to hear them talking, so he took Randall's advice. He inched open all the drawers and doors, but aside from the letters, found only folded bandages.

He stood back and forced himself to think through what he'd discovered so far. His father hadn't stolen the spike, but when a rumour had spread that he had, someone killed him while looking for it. And now, Arnold Jameson was searching for the spike, Myron Cole had died, and this cabinet was one of the few connections between the events of fifteen years ago and now.

Without much hope, Glenn withdrew the letters and glanced through them. When he noticed that many of them were brittle and yellowing with age, he spread them out on the floor. While Randall slipped back to the door, he sat cross-legged and scanned several, finding them to be letters from Brown's friends and relatives and of no interest.

The deeper he delved, the older became the dates on the letters. Glenn was considering giving up reading and searching elsewhere when the handwriting on one letter grabbed his attention.

For long moments he stared at the page, his heart thudding. It didn't include a name, but he was sure he recognized the looping style of the lettering – his sister's.

Thank you for the money, he read. *I am so very pleased that the cabinet is of use to you, and if you wish to take anything else, please do so. I no longer want any involvement with anything to do with that house.*

But in consideration of more appealing matters, I can report that I am settling in far more quickly than I expected I would, and you were most kind to suggest an introduction for me. He has already provided me with a base from which I can start my life anew. And

101

I was lucky in that that one introduction enabled me to secure work along with a home.

You are also most understanding not to refer to a subject which I am uncomfortable in discussing, although with the benefit of so much distance from Black Rock, it no longer feels as important as once it did. So I am sure that . . .

Glenn turned over the page, but there was no writing on the other side. He opened the envelope and searched through the rest of the letters, but he couldn't find the second page.

Randall rejoined him. 'Did those letters help?' he asked.

'Added more confusion than anything,' Glenn said, placing the letters back in the drawer and attempting to arrange them as he'd found them.

Then he searched elsewhere in the room, finding a writing-desk by the wall.

'But you've found something?' Randall asked, following him.

'I don't know yet.' Glenn stopped beside the desk. 'I need to find the rest of a letter first.'

'Just tell me what you've learned so far,' Randall urged and grabbed his arm, but Glenn tore it away and, as his arm flailed, his hand brushed an oil-lamp on the desk.

The lamp rocked, then teetered. He lunged for it but his fingers grasped on air as it fell away from him and crashed to the floor.

Both men stood still, silently frozen in their positions as they embarked on a futile attempt to restore the calm that had reigned before.

Then Glenn heard raised voices in the room next door, followed by Arnold demanding to know what had caused the noise. Footfalls paced towards the door.

They exchanged glances, agreeing silently on a plan of action. They hurried to press themselves against the wall on either side of the door. Glenn saw a triangle of light flood across the floor, then widen as the door swung open.

'What's happening?' Arnold shouted from the main room.

'Nothing that I can see,' the man in the doorway reported.

'Then get in there. I'm sure I heard something.'

While grumbling to himself, the man paced into the room and walked past Glenn and Randall. He didn't look left or right as his gaze centred on the lamp on the floor, then rose to look towards the open window.

Glenn glared across the room at Randall, trying to convey with his eyes that this man might think a breeze from the window had knocked over the lamp and he might not see them in the shadows when he turned. But Randall didn't look at him and instead, he stalked up behind the man, his gun raised high, then clipped the back of his head.

The man collapsed without a sound. Randall caught him before he hit the floor, then manoeuvred him to lie out of sight from the door.

With the door still open, Glenn mouthed a silent comment to Randall that they needed to head out through the window before another person came to investigate, but Randall shook his head and turned to the door instead.

Glenn paced round to stand before him and frantically gestured to the window, trying to impress upon Randall that they'd learnt all they could here and that they now needed to get away. With gestures, he conveyed that too many men were in the next room and they needed to consider their next actions, but Randall walked straight by him towards the door.

He stopped three paces from the door, held his gun high, rolled his shoulders, then charged into the main room.

Glenn watched him disappear from view, then glanced at the window. He shrugged, swirled round and ran through the door after Randall.

CHAPTER 10

Glenn ran doubled up into the room, darting his gaze at each of the men inside. Randall had reacted with sufficient speed to take Arnold and his two men by surprise and they were all still scrambling for their guns as Randall slid to a halt.

As Doc Brown dived for cover, he arced gunfire to his side, scything through the chest of the man who was standing by the window. This man crashed back into the wall before rebounding, but Randall's repeated gunfire tore into his chest and blasted him backwards through the glass, sending shards flying in all directions.

Then Randall hurried into cover behind the large cupboard by the side wall.

Glenn wasn't as sure of himself with a gun as Randall was; when he fired on the run, his gunfire was wild, but he delivered it with sufficient speed to send his targets scurrying for cover behind the table.

Glenn looked around for cover of his own and only saw a chair, its frail woodwork barely adequate, but it was closer than either of the doorways. Glenn hunkered down behind it, reloading.

But he was still slipping slugs from his gunbelt when one of the men risked bobbing up to fire at him. In desperation, Glenn dropped to the floor, but Randall darted out and tore a quick shot at the attacker that winged his shoulder, knocking him back; a second shot wheeled him to the floor.

After that Arnold didn't risk looking up. Long moments passed with Glenn glancing around the sides of the chair, waiting for him to show while wondering whether he should seek better cover.

'Arnold Jameson,' Randall said from the side wall, 'you and I got ourselves a stand-off here.'

'Wrong,' Arnold said. 'You got nothing. I got you pinned down.'

'You ain't. You hired a whole heap of useless dregs to help you, and now they've met the same fate as you will.'

'You got no need to kill me over an argument about a two-hundred-and-fifty-dollar bounty.'

'We both know it ain't about that no more. I know what you're after. I just didn't think even you would kill Myron Cole to get it.'

'I ain't killed nobody. You know I was in Leavenworth when Myron died.'

'I arrived after you. I don't know for sure where you were when Myron died.'

Arnold grunted to himself. 'I'll give you this – I did see him. But he was alive when I left him.'

'Was that because he told you what you wanted to know?'

Arnold chuckled, his voice rising with confidence

for the first time.

'I'm way behind the man who did kill them, but I picked up some clues, like you have. Except you ain't picked up as many as I have.'

'Tell me what else I don't know and you can leave here alive.'

'I will leave, but not on your terms.' Arnold slowly stood and Glenn saw that he was clutching Doc Brown to his chest, his gun pressed into his side. 'Do anything and your friend dies.'

One pace at a time Arnold moved sideways to the door, as, from the other door, his only other surviving accomplice staggered out to follow him with a hand held to his head.

'What you hoping to gain here, Arnold?' Randall shouted.

'Be quiet or Doc Brown gets torn in half.' Arnold dug the gun into Brown's ribs and backed another pace towards the door.

Brown's eyes were blank and Glenn saw no fear in them, only defiance and perhaps. . . ? Brown blinked and a moment before he reacted, Glenn saw what he was about to do. Glenn started to rise, a warning to Randall on his lips, but he was too late – as Arnold back-kicked the door open, he was off balance for a moment. Brown squirmed, then elbowed Arnold in the stomach.

Arnold teetered backwards through the door and Brown managed a single pace towards safety, but from outside, Arnold fired, his bullet tearing into Brown's back. Brown staggered a pace then fell to his knees before sprawling on to his belly, while outside

Arnold hurried away.

This time, Randall was slow to react, the shock of seeing his friend shot rooting him to the spot. It was Glenn who kept his wits about him and fired at Arnold's accomplice. His shots were high and wild but, keeping low, he ran out from the chair to reach the table, then came up underneath it and ran with it held before him. With the table held as a shield, lead cannoned into the wood, but Glenn kept running, slammed the man back against the wall and kept him pinned.

Then another gunshot sounded, and another. Glenn realized that it was coming from behind him. He darted away and even before the table hit the floor, Randall had pumped enough lead into the man to make him slide down the wall to slump, life-less, on the floor.

Then Randall ran past Brown's body and hurried outside without a word.

Glenn moved to follow him, but he accepted that Randall probably didn't want or need his help to catch Arnold. Instead, he knelt beside the doctor. He rolled him on his back. Brown was still breathing but it came in short, pained bursts.

'Tell me what I got to do,' Glenn said. 'Use me to heal yourself.'

'Just make me . . .' A prolonged wince contorted Brown's features. 'Don't bother.'

Glenn considered the blood flowing freely and winced, accepting that Brown probably knew better than anyone that there was nothing even a doctor could do.

'Randall will get Arnold for this.'

'I know.' With just his eyes, Brown pointed to the open door to the adjoining room. 'You saw what was in there?'

'The cabinet, the letter, yeah.'

'Then I'm sorry,' Brown murmured, his eyes closing. 'I guess it was me who introduced them.'

'Introduced who? I don't know what any of this means.'

'You will . . . tomorrow . . . it all happens tomorrow. Clyde Price has asked him to come tomorrow.'

'Who comes tomorrow?' Glenn shook Brown's shoulder, but the doctor gave one long moaning breath, then lay slackly in his grasp. Glenn shook him again, but with the doctor's eyes dimming, he had no choice but to place him on the floor.

He still knelt over him while he tried to work out what he had meant. Then realized he wasn't alone and that Randall was standing in the doorway. He looked up.

'How is he?' Randall asked, his tone gruff.

'It's not worth fetching help.' Glenn watched Randall frown, then nodded over his shoulder. 'And Arnold?'

'He got away.' Randall slapped his holster. 'But it won't do him much good. I'll get him and make him suffer for this.'

'Brown knew that.' Glenn narrowed his eyes and lowered his voice. 'But you didn't pursue him just now when you could have done.'

Randall snorted. 'What you getting at?'

'I mean you could have chased after Arnold and

109

maybe even caught him, but you didn't.' Glenn smiled as Randall snorted his breath through his nostrils and advanced on him. 'And that just means you were worried about your old friend Doc Brown and you had to find out how he was first.'

Randall stopped pacing towards him and shrugged.

'What's that matter?'

Glenn stood. 'It matters because you pretend you don't care about nothing but bringing 'em in for the bounty, but I understand you and I've seen yet again that you care more than you'll admit.'

'And I do, but I care about old friends.' Randall glanced down at Brown, then looked at Glenn and sneered. 'And that doesn't include you.'

'Perhaps it doesn't, but I'll just note that as being another sign that you're capable of caring.'

Randall turned to the door. 'You do that. But now, I got a man to track down. You can do whatever you want because this is where you and I part company.'

'It isn't. I don't reckon you got back in time to hear what Brown said before he died and unless—'

'That's enough!' Randall roared, swirling round and storming towards Glenn. 'I'm not helping you no more and you will tell me what you reckon is happening here.'

Glenn backed away from Randall, but when Randall continued to advance on him, he raised his fists.

'You can try and shake it out of me, but you got no chance.'

Randall considered Glenn's fists, then gave a snorting chuckle.

'Then I'll enjoy myself doing it. Remember, I saw you hiding behind that chair and failing to hit anyone with your wild gunfire.'

'And remember, I still had the courage to take Arnold on. I didn't get much chance to learn how to fight with a gun before I went to Leavenworth, but I sure learnt plenty of other ways to fight in there. Chains, tables, it don't matter to me. I'll take everyone on until I find out who killed my father.'

Randall stopped his pacing and considered Glenn. He shook his head and looked away, sighing. In response Glenn lowered his fists, but then Randall broke into a run, thrust his head down, and slammed into Glenn. He carried him back five paces, Glenn all the time scrambling to get a foothold and stop Randall driving him back towards the wall.

Then he relented and went limp, letting Randall bundle him over, but as he fell, he kicked up. His left foot splayed wide, but his right boot caught Randall with a solid blow to the thigh that made him stumble while still running forward.

Glenn continued to roll out of Randall's way and came up on his feet behind Randall, then hurled himself on his back. As Randall stomped to a halt, Glenn stabbed his fingers at his face aiming for his eyes, but Randall nudged his head out of the way, then hefted Glenn's weight and bodily carried him across the room to the wall. Then he spun round and threw himself back against the wall.

Trapped between Randall's heavy back and the

wall, all the air blasted out of Glenn's lungs. It hadn't returned when Randall slammed him back a second and a third time. Glenn's arms went slack and he fell from Randall's back, then looked up to see a boot heading straight for his face.

He rocked his head back but it still crunched into his forehead. Blackness descended.

A timeless period later a cold splash in the face and a persistent slapping of his cheeks brought him back to consciousness.

He opened his eyes to see that Randall had pinned him back against the wall and was holding him tightly. The bucket of water at his feet said he had blacked out for at least several minutes, but the wide-eyed and reddened face confronting him said that Randall's anger hadn't abated.

'You may have learnt how to fight dirty in Leavenworth,' Randall said, 'but I bring in the men who have learned how to fight dirty. Now tell me everything you know and you can live long enough to get out of my sight.'

'Randall, we still need each other. We can sort this out together but only—'

Randall flared his eyes, a touch of something, perhaps grim humour in his gaze.

'But only if you're still alive come *tomorrow*.'

'Tomorrow . . . You did hear what Brown said.'

'But only you know what it means.'

Glenn glanced down at Randall's fist and raised his eyebrows. Randall held on for a moment longer, then released him with a snap of his hand and stood back.

Glenn shrugged his jacket and collar while he stood and composed himself enough to think through what Brown's comment could have meant. He reckoned he was close to understanding it, but there were still vital clues missing.

'Sheriff Emerson Price is helping Arnold Jameson to search for the spike and he's getting closer because Myron Cole saw something that accidentally revealed where it was and perhaps even the identity of the man who killed my father. I missed it, but Adam Price knew what it was, so he spoke up for me.'

'And he died three months ago.'

'Yeah. And before he died, he told Emerson what he knew, so the sheriff called for Arnold and he started working through everyone connected to the events of fifteen years ago. His quest took him through the witness and then to me and then to the man who owned the cabinet that once hid the spike.'

'And the next man on his list arrives in Black Rock tomorrow?'

'Yeah.'

'And who is he?'

Glenn considered whether he should keep his assumption to himself, but the act of talking had helped him put his thoughts in order and he found that he didn't want to keep his thoughts private any more.

'The last person I spoke to before I found my father's body – Senator Matlock Langhorne. And as he's an important person, he'll arrive on the train.'

'Obliged to you for that and for explaining your-self, eventually.' Randall tipped his hat and backed away to the door, but Glenn raised a hand halting him.

'That mean you're going after Arnold now?'

'Sure am.'

'But I plan to board that train and see Matlock for myself.'

Randall shrugged. 'Don't care what you do. I'm going after Arnold.'

'You can, but think about this.' Glenn smiled. 'What better way is there to catch Arnold than to be with the man Arnold will be after?'

CHAPTER 11

Late in the morning, Glenn and Randall slipped on to the platform at Greengate City to await the train to Black Rock.

Even though they were fifty miles from Black Rock, Glenn was worried that anyone might recognize him, so he lurked beside the station wall and avoided meeting anyone's eye. Even when the train arrived, he stayed in the shadows. Only when all the passengers had boarded the train and it was ready to move out did he join Randall in the rear car.

Glenn was thankful that, overnight and this morning, Randall hadn't pressed Glenn for many details as to why he believed Matlock Langhorne was coming to Black Rock by train, accepting that his hunches were as good as any. And in his silence, Glenn had detected a hint of respect that he had pieced together what was happening more readily than Randall had.

Glenn was unsure as to why he welcomed gaining the respect of a man who had twice captured him and who, despite Glenn's attempts to explain his actions as being those of a decent man, still insisted they were working together only out of convenience.

But still, Glenn was pleased that they were still working together and that he had someone's help in unravelling the events of fifteen years ago to find, he hoped, the man who had murdered his father.

As soon as the train lurched to a start, Randall and Glenn made their way through the cars. They walked through the first two without seeing Matlock, and Glenn started to worry as to whether he'd be able to recognize a man who had had a complete change in life style since he'd last seen him.

And when they'd walked through the third, and penultimate, car Randall was starting to glare at him and add to his doubts. Then Glenn narrowed his eyes as he looked down the aisle of the last car.

At the end, four people had taken up residence in a double seat. A bonnet indicated that one of those people was a woman. The individual sitting opposite her and facing Glenn had the tailored suit and waxed moustache of a wealthy man. The men sitting on the outside of the seats had the prominent guns and surly glares of hired guns.

The hired gun facing Glenn had already sized them up as being potential trouble and was whispering to his colleague, who rolled his head around the side of the seat to consider them. Their movement caused the man and the woman to shuffle in their seats and the woman raised herself for a moment to look over her shoulder, then flopped back into her seat.

Glenn gulped, his mind whirling, and when

Randall turned to him, he ignored him and just stared down the aisle with his mouth wide open. Then, with every step feeling unreal, he set off down the aisle, his gait long and his eyes wide open and staring. Randall grabbed his arm and urged him to be careful, but Glenn shrugged him off, then broke into a run.

'Katie,' he said, his voice breaking, then shouted out his plea. 'Katie, it's me.'

The woman looked back, her eyes wide, but by then the two hired guns had stood and blocked Glenn's path.

'Glenn Price, if I'm not mistaken,' the nearest one said. He glanced at the gun he'd drawn in a fluid motion as he stood. 'Put those hands high.'

'That's my sister,' Glenn said, rocking to the side to peer around him. 'I'd never hurt her. Please let me speak to—'

The second hired gun strode a long pace, lunged out and grabbed Glenn's shoulder. In seconds, he'd frisked him, thrown his gun to the floor, then swung him round to hold him firm against his chest, forcing Glenn to arch his back as a weapon dug into his back.

The first hired gun trained his gun on Randall and signified with a raised eyebrow that doing anything but remove his gun would result in instant death.

Randall did as ordered. With his hands held palm up and level with his shoulders, he took a pace down the aisle until he faced the moustached man in the corner of the seat.

'Whatever you may have heard about Glenn's actions from Sheriff Price, you are mistaken, Senator

Langhorne.'

The man in the corner nodded as Randall correctly identified him, then narrowed his eyes.

'I can remember only bad things about Katie's worthless brother, but you're Randall Nash, aren't you? The man who brought this dastardly outlaw to justice?'

'I am at that, Senator, but now I believe him to be innocent of the crimes everyone claims he committed.'

Langhorne considered Randall, then nodded. 'I believed you to be an honourable man when you brought Glenn in the first time. So I will trust your word, but that doesn't mean either of you will get your guns back. And if Glenn upsets Katie, I will have him thrown from the train.'

With a snap of the wrist, the hired gun released Glenn and pushed him forward to stand before the seat. Glenn and Katie looked at each other. Shock, surprise, embarrassment and some consternation registered in her open-mouthed, aghast expression. Glenn presumed he presented the same impression to her.

Katie was the first to speak. 'I've ... I've never doubted you were innocent and no matter how worried Matlock is, I know you wouldn't hurt me.'

'I wouldn't.' Glenn gulped. 'Is Matlock your ... your husband?'

'He is. And he's a fair man and will help you in any way he can, no matter if you don't want that help.'

'But I do.'

'Then why did you ignore my letters?'

'I didn't. You never wrote to me.'

'I did. Every month in the first year, then so many times after that, but with you not returning them, I just thought . . .'

'You should have just thought of the truth. I never received them. The guards don't treat you like human beings in there.'

She closed her eyes and placed a hand to her heart, breathing deeply.

'You must have suffered badly, but the things I've heard about you. They say you're getting your revenge on the people who put you away.'

'I'm not. Myron Cole died while I was in jail. I'm being framed and I know why. Arnold Jameson has joined forces with Sheriff Price to—'

'Sheriff Emerson Price,' Matlock said, the quiet authority in his tone silencing Glenn, 'wouldn't be behind anything like that. The Prices are an honourable family and you should let some of their honour rub off on you.'

'With all respect, Senator, this honourable family told half-truths at my trial and—'

Matlock raised a hand. 'I understand your anger, but you will say no more. I have been invited to Black Rock to support the son of my old friend Adam Price and to show that a senator is behind him in his quest to become mayor. And to let my wife see her brother before—'

'You brought Katie with you because Clyde Price got in touch and said I'd been arrested for killing Myron Cole, didn't you?'

'I did.'

'And he made that request before Emerson had

even arrested me. He assumed I'd leave jail last week, but I was late in leaving and—'

Matlock narrowed his eyes, then flicked his gaze to one of his hired guns, the gesture confirming before he spoke that he wouldn't accept any more criticism of Emerson's actions.

'That is enough. I am sure everything has a simple explanation. And although I am pleased that maybe Katie's brother isn't the worthless specimen I remember, you will not disparage the Prices again.' Matlock stared at Glenn until he nodded, then gestured to the empty seats on the other side the aisle. 'Now, you might like to sit with your sister and talk. You must have much to catch up on.'

Glenn did as requested and sat in the seat on the other side of the aisle. Katie patted her husband's hand, then sat in the seat facing him. They both leaned forward and held each other's hands.

'Answer me this,' Glenn said. 'Do you believe I didn't kill our father?'

'I've always known that.'

Glenn breathed a sigh of relief. 'And that means somebody else did, and he has never paid for his crime.'

'He hasn't, but bearing ill-will for this long is wrong. You've suffered terribly, but you can still make a fresh start. I have faith that the man who did kill him will face his own Judgment Day without you destroying yourself.'

'I don't have your faith. I need to resolve what happened fifteen years ago because it's playing to an end now.'

'I want to believe you, but you're asking me to persuade my husband to abandon the sons of his old friend. I can't do that without proof.'

'I can't provide that, but I do know Doc Brown effectively helped you and Matlock wed by suggesting you sought him out when you moved East.' Glenn watched Katie nod, then lowered his voice. 'And he's dead.'

Katie threw her hand to her mouth. 'As well?'

'Yes. Arnold Jameson killed him, just like he killed Myron Cole, and just like he'll try to kill Matlock.'

Katie stared hard at Glenn, then shuffled across the aisle to sit opposite Matlock, who looked at her with kindness but also a firmness that gave Glenn no hope he'd listen.

'I heard what Glenn just said,' Matlock said, 'and I've never shied from danger before. I won't start today.'

Katie shot a beseeching glance at Glenn, who joined her.

'I understand that,' he said, 'but I fear for your life.'

The hired guns grunted behind him, and Matlock glanced at them with a hint of humour twinkling in his eyes.

'I thank you for your concern, but as you can see I have protection.'

'Perhaps you're not concerned about yourself, but do be about Katie. Arnold is searching for some information from fifteen years ago, perhaps something minor that was mentioned in my trial that we all forgot.'

'But what information can that be?' Matlock said, frowning as if he did know what the answer might be before he replaced it with a disarming smile. This encouraged Glenn to lean forward and watch Matlock's eyes as he provided the only piece of information he thought might shock him.

'Arnold is searching for the golden spike.'

'But . . .' Matlock's right eye flickered and he turned to look through the window while fingering his moustache.

Glenn sat beside Katie, confident now that Matlock had shown sufficient surprise to mean that he might have information on its whereabouts. He waited, hoping his silence would persuade Matlock to reveal more, but Matlock was a consummate politician and he quickly regained his composure.

'Then perhaps he isn't trying to find it,' Glenn said eventually. He pressed his cheek to the glass to peer ahead. 'But either way, we'll find out soon enough. We're approaching Black Rock.'

'In that case,' Matlock said, 'I have no choice as to what I must do. I hope you'll support my decision.'

Five minutes later the train pulled into the station. Glenn had already shuffled down in his seat and pulled his hat low, and could only watch the roofs of the buildings then the station glide into view as the train drew to a halt. As Matlock stood and muttered final instructions to his hired guns, Glenn looked at Katie.

'You sure about this?' he asked.

'I am,' she said. 'Just stay on the train and let Matlock do the talking.'

'Then just you stay on the train,' Glenn said, 'and stay out of trouble.'

Katie shook her head. 'I will stay with my husband. Whatever danger he may face, I will too.'

Matlock was in the midst of moving from his seat, but he sat back on the seat beside her and held her hand.

'In this, I agree with your brother. If Arnold is determined to cause me trouble, he could try to harm you. Stay close and don't go into town on your own.'

Katie opened her mouth to argue but with Matlock on one side and Glenn on the other looking at her and shaking their heads, she gave a reluctant nod. Then Matlock gathered his two hired guns around him, smoothed his jacket, slapped his hat on his head, and left the train.

Randall stayed back to acknowledge Glenn, then followed him.

A huge cheer arose as Matlock emerged on to the platform. As Glenn was sitting slumped in his seat to avoid being seen from outside, Katie had to inform him of Matlock's passage across the platform and towards a podium that had been set up beside the station house.

When Katie informed him that everyone had cleared away from the platform, Glenn felt safe enough to sit up in his seat. By now, Matlock had started his speech and the orchestrated applause and cheers of the townsfolk rippled across the platform to him.

His speech was as dull as Glenn would have expected from a politician. It spoke of his support for his home town, his assurance that the son of his old friend Adam Price would make a fine mayor and that the townsfolk were the finest people he'd ever met. He even promised a substantial donation to the town, a declaration that earned him the largest cheer so far and everyone's complete attention.

As the speech continued, Glenn stood and headed to the door. Katie joined him and together they listened while staying out of sight of anyone who might pass along the platform.

Glenn was just suppressing a yawn when the speech took its scheduled divergence.

'But there is one thing I stand for and for which I am sure this town stands,' Matlock announced, 'and that is the need for justice . . .'

Matlock paused for just long enough to receive a cheer.

'. . . the need for truth . . .' Another cheer. '. . . and the need to accept that any man, no matter what his background, needs to receive that justice.'

Another loud cheer echoed.

'And so it pains me to say that this town failed to give the wayward brother of my very own wife a second chance . . .' Matlock paused, but if he was expecting a cheer, one didn't arrive. 'I have heard that yesterday a mob tried to lynch Glenn Price on grounds based on nothing more than a rumour.'

Somebody shouted, but the words were unintelligible to Glenn, and in the train he flashed a worried frown at Katie. She returned an encouraging smile and a mouthed plea to trust her husband.

'You are quite right, my friend,' Matlock contin-

124

ued. 'Glenn was tried and sentenced for the murder of my very own father-in-law, a crime that pains me more than it pains any of you. But he has served his time and I can find it in my heart to forgive him. If I can do that, why can't you?'

The heckler shouted back and Glenn heard Myron Cole's name uttered amongst others.

'And from what I have heard, Myron Cole died while Glenn was still serving his sentence in Leavenworth. Does it sound as if he is guilty?'

Glenn winced, steeling himself, and he did hear several argumentative heckles, but he was pleased to hear a few grunts of approval.

'Glenn Price,' Sheriff Price said from closer to the podium, 'still has a case to face.'

'And he does, but not from a lynch mob. And while you continue to pursue the increasingly unlikely possibility that Glenn is guilty, the real culprit walks amongst us, threatening us all. I stand by Glenn Price, and so should all of you.'

Glenn took a deep breath. Matlock was close to delivering the cue for him to show himself, provided he had talked everyone around, and he looked at Katie.

'If you're going to do it,' she said, 'you won't get a better chance than now.'

Glenn nodded then returned to listening. He heard Matlock mention his pride in his home town. He took a deep breath and, after exchanging a quick hug with Katie, he opened the door and jumped down on to the platform. With her at his side and his head held high, he strode across the deserted platform, to the podium and then the crowd beyond opened up to his view.

At first, nobody looked his way, but then the towns-folk before the podium shuffled round to look at him, a ripple of grunted irritation and disbelief rising up. Matlock chose that moment to look back and hold his arm out, inviting Glenn to join him.

Glenn gave Katie a last hug and whispered to her to stay here behind the podium, then hurried on to the podium. He joined Matlock, who thrust out his hand. Glenn took that hand and returned the hearty handshake, then cast his gaze across the crowd.

He couldn't say that many people met his eye, but he took that as a sign of shame and not of the festering anger of yesterday. At the front of the crowd, the Price brothers were glaring at him, but down the road, outside the hotel, Niles and Hop had brought Stewart outside. Niles nodded towards him, smiling. Hop was still scowling and Stewart was sitting slumped and possibly asleep in his chair.

'And now,' Matlock said, turning back to the crowd, 'that I have shown my willingness to forgive Glenn Price, I hope you all can too. And under Mayor Clyde Price, this town will deserve its reputation as a town where the townsfolk have courage and integrity.'

Matlock backed away, waving at several members of the crowd, who with a speed that suggested they had been paid to do so, waved back, then started clapping. The applause grew, but only slowly until the prospective mayor, Clyde Price, took the podium and waved for quiet.

126

'Thank you, my old friend, Senator Matlock Langhorne,' he began. His gaze drifted over Glenn, pausing to sneer before he returned to looking at the crowd. He resumed his speech.

Sheriff Price followed his brother on to the podium, his gaze boring into Glenn. Matlock intercepted him, then nudged past him and joined Glenn, ensuring that he stood between him and the Price brothers.

'That was better received than I feared it might be,' he said from the corner of his mouth.

'And I'm obliged that you spoke up for me,' Glenn said. 'It couldn't have been—'

'—easy,' Sheriff Price said, darting behind Matlock to slap a firm hand on Glenn's shoulder. He slipped in between the two men then looked up to face the crowd, giving a wide smile that didn't sit well with his grunted words. 'Now quit the politician's garble and tell me why you've made it well-nigh impossible for me to arrest this runt?'

'Because he is innocent,' Matlock said.

'He is not. And no amount of fine words will convince me of that.'

Glenn snorted. 'I wasn't even—'

Matlock raised a hand, silencing him. 'Continue to smile, gentlemen, while we are standing on the podium. I want everyone to see we are all good friends here.'

As Clyde continued to deliver his speech, Matlock waved at several nearby people. Glenn attempted to match Matlock's generous smile, but Emerson made no such attempt.

'We are not friends,' he snapped. 'So talk without using any of that politician's double-talk. Why did you support him?'

'It is of no concern of yours,' Matlock said, while still smiling and waving, 'but if you want plain speaking, I will remind you that I have bankrolled the Price family for the last fifteen years. Without me, Adam would have achieved nothing and your brother wouldn't be in a position to become mayor, no matter how good he is at making speeches. And if either of you has any ambitions beyond this pathetic dung heap, you will need friends like me. Do I make myself clear, Sheriff?'

Matlock flashed a harsh glare at Emerson, then snapped round to face the front and gave a huge smile.

Emerson snapped a curt nod. 'Perfectly clear.'

Behind them, the train rattled out of the station, the noise temporarily halting Clyde's speech. In the break, Matlock lowered his voice and talked rapidly to Emerson.

'And here's more clarity. Your hatred of Glenn motivated your method of allocating blame for Myron's murder. But you need a new man to arrest now and one name is obvious – Arnold Jameson. I suggest when Clyde has finished talking, you announce that Arnold is the man you want.'

Emerson glanced away as he rubbed his chin.

'He couldn't have killed Myron. He was—'

'But you have one solid fact,' Glenn said. 'He killed Doc Brown.'

'Brown is dead?' Emerson said, speaking to Glenn

128

using a civil tone for the first time.

Glenn was surprised to see Emerson's eyes open wide in apparent shock. With a grunted oath to himself, Emerson turned and craned his neck as he peered down the road, then paced round on the spot, running his gaze across the nearest buildings.

'So Arnold *is* in town,' Glenn said. 'You did hire him. You knew he'd try to kill Matlock, and you were going to let him.'

'Be quiet,' Emerson grunted. 'I may not be able to hang you now but that doesn't mean I have to listen to your wild theories.'

Glenn followed the direction of Emerson's gaze, also searching for where in town Arnold could have hidden himself. Then he noticed that Matlock was also looking around, his gaze repeatedly returning to behind the podium and the station house. Then Matlock's eyes narrowed and he swirled round to look at his hired guns who were standing on either side of the podium and watching the crowd.

Glenn suddenly realized what had concerned Matlock. He peered over the back of the podium. Katie should be waiting to join her husband for his closing comments, but she wasn't on the platform.

Glenn barged Emerson aside and vaulted over the back of the podium. The only place she could have gone to was into the station house. With a growing pain gnawing at his guts he hurried to the building and threw back the station door. The room was deserted. Katie had gone.

CHAPTER 12

Still unable to accept that Katie had gone, Glenn hurried around the station house, kicking over chairs and toppling a table, before he returned to the deserted platform.

Matlock and Randall arrived a moment later, with the hired guns trailing in their wake and looking in all directions.

'Arnold took her?' Matlock bleated.

'Yeah,' Glenn said. 'Perhaps he wanted to get you originally, but I guess he's decided that kidnapping her might still get him what he wants.'

'But where has he gone?'

Glenn paced across the platform until he reached the tracks, then stared away from the town.

If Arnold had stayed in town, surely somebody would have seen him and his victim, so he must have left. As he'd only had a few minutes in which to effect Katie's kidnapping, he should still be visible.

Then movement to the side drew Glenn's attention and he looked down the tracks at the receding train.

'He's on the train,' he said.

'You can't know that. It's a big hunch. If we follow the train, it could give him time to get away.'

'It could,' Randall said, slapping Glenn's back. 'But I'm learning to trust this man's instincts. I'm going after the train.'

Glenn stayed just long enough to acknowledge Randall's declaration. Then with Matlock's help, they secured horses and in good speed headed out of town. By now the train had built up to its full speed and was hurtling away from town, so they both had to ride at a gallop to close on it.

Matlock's doubts about Glenn's hunch encouraged the hired guns to employ a more measured pace and they took the opportunity to glance around, searching the plains for Arnold and Katie. This let Randall and Glenn hurry on ahead to reach the train first. They swung in to keep close to the tracks to avoid Arnold being able to see them and exchanged brief comments about their tactics.

Curiously, despite being worried for his sister's safety, Glenn was relaxed, enjoying working as an equal with Randall for the first time.

They were at least a half-mile ahead of Matlock and his hired guns when they matched the speed of the train. Sheriff Price had stayed behind to organize a posse and his group was only just leaving town.

Glenn swung in towards the rear car. He rehearsed his actions in his mind several times, then stood tall in the saddle and leapt from his horse. Just as he had done when leaping from the balcony yesterday, he slammed into the back rail and grabbed hold. He hung there for a moment, his body folded over the rail, then rolled over it to stand on the back of the car. Then he waited with his hands outstretched for Randall to attempt the tricky manoeuvre.

Randall matched the speed of the train, then launched himself at the car, but he didn't need Glenn's help as he grabbed the ladder to the train roof with one hand and the rail with the other. He steadied himself, then vaulted the rail to stand beside Glenn.

'Which carriage do you reckon he's in?' Randall asked.

'He'll have to stay out of everyone's way,' Glenn said while opening the door, 'so I reckon he might hide in—'

The door burst open and lead tore through the doorway, two brisk shots whistling by Glenn, the third tearing into the doorframe. Glenn darted back to stand to the side of the door.

Randall offered a low laugh. 'Were you about to say he'd be in the rear car?'

'I wasn't. But I guess I've proved where he is.'

Glenn risked glancing into the darkened interior, seeing that this car didn't have windows and the only light inside came through the open door.

'Arnold will be waiting for us to come in through the door,' he said, patting the ladder on the back of the car. 'We need to surprise him. I'll head over the roof and come at him from the other side.'

Randall nodded and stood aside, letting Glenn climb up the ladder. He quickly reached the roof and stood with his hands outstretched co-ordinating his movements with the rolling of the train, then he set off. Halfway along the car he paused to crouch and look back towards Black Rock. He saw that a quarter-mile back a sprawling line of riders was following. He discerned Matlock and his hired guns at the front of the group, but he judged them to be too far away to help for a while.

Then he continued across the roof, picking his steps with care. He didn't think Arnold would be able to hear his footfalls over the rattling of the train, but he still walked as slowly and as quietly as he could.

At the far end he moved to climb down the ladder, then flinched back. Down below was Arnold and he was dragging Katie through the doorway. Glenn ventured another glance and found that he was looking into Arnold's eyes. He flicked his hand towards his gun, but Arnold moved his gun to the side to aim it at Katie's chest, giving a warning shake of his head.

'What do you hope to get out of this?' Glenn shouted.

'She knows where the spike is,' Arnold said.

'She doesn't. You reckon you've worked it all out, but you're wrong.'

'I don't reckon so and now you'll warn everyone off.' Arnold swung his gun round to aim through the door. 'And step back, Randall.'

He stared into the car, then gave a short nod that implied Randall had backed away. He pushed Katie up the ladder, following her until he reached the roof. Then he dragged her along the top and away from Glenn.

Glenn stepped back three paces, broke into a run

133

and jumped over the gap to the next car. He immediately stopped his forward motion as Arnold
grunted a warning. For several minutes they faced
each other. Arnold stood halfway down the roof
clutching Katie to his chest, his lips curled back in a
savage sneer. Katie kept her resolute gaze on Glenn,
who returned that gaze as softly as he could, conveying that everything would be fine.

Eventually Arnold broke the frozen tableau by
glancing sideways. Glenn turned to see that Matlock
and his hired guns had reached the train on horse-
back and were matching its speed. As he rode along,
Matlock was peering up at the confrontation taking
place on the train roof, and even from some distance
Glenn could see the anguish contorting his face.
Then Glenn turned to concentrate on Arnold,
watching him start to back away with Katie held to
him. In his grasp, Katie was still surprisingly calm,
keeping her head high and her back straight as
Arnold dragged her backwards.

'You don't want to do this,' Glenn said, raising his
hands slightly so as to appear unthreatening as he
advanced on Arnold. 'You wouldn't have captured
her if you wanted to kill her. If you keep threatening
her, the only thing that'll happen here is that you'll
die.'

Arnold sneered and darted his gaze over Glenn's
head. Glenn strained his hearing and heard Randall
clambering up the ladder. The hand with which
Arnold was holding Katie started to shake as he
looked to Glenn, then to Matlock and then to his
hired guns riding beside the tracks.

'I guess you're right,' he said, gulping. 'I bet Matlock's hired guns have the accuracy to kill me without even getting on the train.'

'That's mighty sensible talk,' Glenn said, nodding. He held his hands wide, gave Katie an encouraging smile, which she returned, then turned back to Arnold. 'It's time to give up.'

'It is, but I ain't a man to give up.' Arnold treated Glenn to a huge grin then swung Katie away from his chest and hurled her towards the edge of the train.

Glenn uttered an involuntary cry of anguish, but Arnold still had a tight grip of her arm as he fell to his knees. Her foot slipped over the edge and Arnold encouraged her to slip further by shoving her. She rolled over the side, dragging him with her, but he braced himself and halted her fall, stopping himself with him lying on his side, both hands clasping Katie's arm.

She dangled below him, her feet scrambling for purchase on the side of the train.

'What did you do that for?' Glenn shouted.

'Ensuring I get what I want,' Arnold shouted, a maniacal gleam in his eye. 'I haven't got a gun on her now, but if anyone shoots me, I'll lose my grip and she'll hit the ground before I die.'

Glenn glanced over the side of the train at Matlock and waved frantically, demanding that his hired guns didn't fire. They did draw back slightly and when Matlock joined Glenn in ordering them not to fire, they holstered their guns. Glenn breathed a sigh of relief and turned to look down at Arnold.

'Now,' he said, 'pull her back on to the roof.

They're not threatening you no more.'

'They aren't,' said Arnold, looking up at and beyond Glenn. 'But he is.'

Glenn realized he was looking at Randall, who was now approaching slowly from behind. He listened to Randall's slow deliberate paces as he came to Glenn's side, his gun drawn and aimed down at Arnold.

'You'll die whatever happens to Katie,' Randall said, his voice low and demanding. 'And you won't get the spike. And you won't get no bounty. You will just die.'

'Randall,' Glenn urged, rolling on to his side to look up at Randall, 'quit the demands. We can talk this through.'

'We can't,' Randall grunted without taking his resolute gaze off Arnold. 'Ready to die yet, Arnold?'

'Don't risk it,' Glenn shouted. 'Katie's life is worth more than the spike, more than any of this.'

'And you'll stop ordering me around,' Randall grunted. 'Now, Arnold. Before, when you held Doc Brown, I hesitated, but not this time. It's just between you and me. The woman don't matter, the bounty don't matter, the spike don't matter. One of us dies here. Which one of us is it going to be?'

Arnold gulped, but then with a great roar of defiance he swung up his right arm, aiming his gun towards Randall. Glenn saw that with Arnold taking action there was no chance of talking Randall into not taking him on. He broke into a run as Randall fired, his single shot slamming straight between Arnold's eyes, knocking him on his back, his arms and legs splaying wide.

A scream erupted from beneath the rim of the roof as Arnold's hand released his grip of Katie's arm. He saw her arm snake over the side as she fell, her clawed fingers failing to grip the roof of the train, but still Glenn threw himself to the roof and slid across the timbers. His outstretched hand reached for a hand that was no longer there and his desperate lunge fell short by feet of the edge.

With nothing but forlorn hope in his heart, he wriggled to the edge and half-threw himself over the side, praying that she'd somehow defied gravity by catching on to a projection. But he couldn't see her below and he pressed his forehead to the roof of the train, unable to look back down the tracks and see her broken body lying there.

Randall slapped a hand on his back and moved to hoist him up, but Glenn squirmed and batted the hand away.

'You got your revenge on Arnold,' he screeched. 'But you got her killed. You got the only member of my family—'

'Saved.' Randall lunged down, dragged Glenn to his feet and pointed over his shoulder. 'I got her saved.'

'Saved?' Glenn stared back at Randall then wrested himself free to look over the side. Riding to a halt some 200 yards back down the tracks was Matlock with Katie slung over the side of his horse. 'She landed on his horse?'

'She sure did.'

'But how. . . ? Why. . . ?'

'I didn't shoot Arnold until I saw that Matlock had

137

moved in to ride below her.' Randall patted Glenn's back. 'It's a pity you didn't realize just how decent a man I am.'

Glenn sighed with relief. 'You could have let me know.'

Randall shrugged then gave a slow wink.

'I needed you to not see what was happening below so you could convince Arnold I'd kill him if he didn't take me on. And you did a good job of appearing right shocked.' Randall swirled his gun back into his holster and turned away.

'Then I was right,' Glenn said. 'You do care about something more than just bringing 'em in for the bounty.'

Randall stopped for a moment then continued walking to the end of the car.

Five minutes after rescuing Katie, Randall persuaded the conductor to halt the train, enabling them to disembark and return to town. The strung-out posse had arrived by then and accompanied them on their journey. For the first time many of these people acknowledged Glenn with curt nods and those who didn't look at him appeared to be too embarrassed to catch his eye.

But as Sheriff Price was one of the people who didn't look at him, Glenn reckoned his problems in Black Rock weren't at an end just yet.

When they returned to town many of the group who had chased after the train headed to the saloon. Matlock promised to join them and buy everyone a celebratory drink later, leaving just himself, Katie,

Glenn, Randall and the Prices to stand outside the sheriff's office and confirm what had happened.

Further down the road, the Archers stayed outside to watch developments.

In a matter-of-fact manner Randall provided a brief testimony of the day's events, after which Sheriff Price declared himself happy to conclude that Arnold had killed both Myron Cole and Doc Brown in his misguided quest for the golden spike. But when he turned to question Glenn, all signs of his reasonable demeanour disappeared as he glared at him. He dragged him a few paces away from the rest of the group and barked out his complaints.

'Don't go thinking I've forgotten about you. I know you had something to do with Myron's death.' He glanced around to confirm that Senator Langhorne and Katie were out of earshot. 'And I will prove it one day when your friends aren't around to speak up for you. Then I'll come for you.'

Glenn returned Emerson's contempt with his own cold-eyed glare.

'If you're admitting you'll do that, then why don't you quit the pretence and just tell me the whole truth?'

Emerson set his hands on his hips. 'What whole truth?'

'You know the full story behind Arnold's attempt to find the spike, don't you? You know who hired him, who covered up for his killing, who helped him every step of the way, and who enticed Matlock and Katie here to try to learn more about the spike.'

'I've got no idea what you mean.'

139

'I guess you got to keep saying that. After all, a lawman can't arrest himself.' Glenn watched Emerson flinch back, sneering. 'I can't prove that, but somehow I will prove that your corruption is turning this town into something no decent person can enjoy.' Glenn pointed down the road to the Archer hotel. 'If only the Prices had a tenth of the decency of the Archers, this would all be different.'

'The Prices *are* decent,' Emerson snorted. 'You are either demented or confused. But either way, you have no evidence to make accusations like that. And if you persist with them, I will kill you, whether I can prove you're guilty or not.'

'And I guess the same goes for me. You got no evidence to prove your accusations. So keep them to yourself.'

Emerson shook his head. 'Unlike you, I have evidence. Remember, I have a witness who saw you kill Myron.'

'Another person in the pay of the Prices, I suppose?'

'No, it was someone I hate. And I can't wait to see your expression when I tell you who it is.' Emerson gave a wide smile and turned to look down the road towards the hotel. 'The man who claimed he saw you kill Myron Cole was the man you claim is an ally – Hop Archer.'

140

CHAPTER 13

Glenn staggered back a pace before he turned to stare down the road at the Archer family standing outside the hotel. Hop couldn't possibly have heard Emerson's declaration, but he was sure he saw him grin, and in that moment Glenn realized the truth.

'Adam did tell you about the spike before he died, but Stewart also told Hop what he suspected.' He swung round to face Emerson. 'Your hatred of me has blinded you to the simple truth that Hop killed Myron.'

'I ain't listening to this madness,' Emerson turned to walk away, but Glenn grabbed his arm, halting him.

'Then think of this,' he muttered. 'Myron was the only witness to what happened fifteen years ago, but maybe he lied to cover up the truth that he stole the spike and killed my father.'

'Myron was a decent man.'

'And he was also the man who forged the spike. Perhaps all those long hours working with the gold twisted his mind and he wanted it for himself.'

'Release me. Nothing you can say will convince me.'

'Then just accept one fact. I couldn't have shot Myron and if Hop is prepared to lie about that, what is he covering up if it's not that he was searching for the spike?'

Glenn fixed Emerson with his firm gaze and it was Emerson who looked away. Then he snorted and headed off down the road towards the hotel. He collected Clyde Price, only stopping to murmur a brief order to him.

Glenn paced after him until he joined the remaining group. Katie and Matlock were still talking quietly to each other. Randall was giving them space and he joined Glenn.

'What was that all about?' he asked.

'I was just explaining what's been happening in this town.'

Randall nodded. 'Then I'd be obliged if you'd explain it to me.'

'Why? I thought you only cared about bringing 'em in for the bounty?'

'I do, but I'm trying to work out whether I might get anything out of this.'

Glenn shrugged. 'To be honest, I got no idea what's been happening for sure.' He pointed down the road to where Clyde and Emerson were swinging round to confront Hop and Niles. 'But I got me a feeling we'll find out the truth any moment now.'

Randall turned to see the long overdue, but currently silent confrontation starting up between the Price and the Archer brothers. Katie and Matlock broke off from their quiet chat to watch also.

'Hop Archer,' Emerson said, further down the road. 'You are under arrest.'

'Why?' Hop said, standing easily.

'Just come quietly and we'll talk about this inside.'

'No need to conduct this behind closed doors. That may be the way of the Prices, but it ain't our way.'

Emerson shook his head. He flexed his right hand and moved it closer to his holster.

Hop matched his action, forcing Emerson to flare his eyes and making Clyde back away a pace, although he also moved his hand towards his holster.

Niles was standing beside his father, who was now awake beneath the blanket drawn up to his chin and was watching developments with an intrigued gleam in his eye. Niles patted his shoulder then walked two slow paces forward.

'Let's not be too hasty over this,' he said, his tone light but forced as he smiled. 'Hop will come with you if that's what you want, but first, tell us in the open what your accusation is.'

'If you insist,' Emerson announced. 'There ain't nobody I hate more than Glenn Price, but I got to admit that when Myron Cole died he was in Leavenworth. So how come Hop says he saw Glenn shoot Myron?'

'Hop says . . .' Niles swirled round to confront Hop, who darted his gaze at each man in turn, his hands shaking, his fingers twitching towards his holster.

'Don't go for that gun,' Emerson warned, 'or

you'll die where you stand.'

'What's this about, Hop?' Niles demanded as Hop continued to inch his fingers in towards his holster.

In response, Emerson steadied his stance and inched his own hand towards his holster, Clyde at his side matching his actions.

'The golden spike,' Emerson said, 'has surfaced again, and Hop reckoned Myron knew where it was.'

Niles snorted then swung round to face Emerson and Clyde.

'That spike is long gone and you won't arrest him over that nonsense.'

Clyde moved round to confront Niles. For long frozen moments the two men faced each other while to their side Hop and Emerson faced each other. Each man watched the other, waiting for one man to make the first move and so bring to a bloody end the feud that had simmered between these two families for years.

But when the first movement came, it came from further down the road. It was Katie who disentangled herself from Matlock's arm and set off down the road, Matlock not even moving to stop her.

'Stay away from them,' Glenn shouted after her.

She turned. 'I'm the only one who can stop this gunfight.'

Glenn broke into a run as she set off and to his surprise Matlock blocked his way and grabbed his arms.

'She's right,' he said. 'She knows the truth.'

'What truth?' Glenn demanded, but Matlock shook his head and turned with him to face down the road.

144

Glenn's warning had now distracted the brothers and they inched back slightly to watch Katie approach.

She stopped ten paces away from Emerson and Hop.

'Stop this,' she said, her voice calm. 'This has nothing to do with the golden spike. That was a distraction Adam and Stewart dreamed up to keep you all occupied and to keep the more important secret buried.'

Behind Hop and Niles, Stewart became animated, waving his bony arms beneath his blanket, but none of the group looked at him.

'Stay out of this,' Emerson said. 'I'm arresting this varmint.'

'But you don't want to do that. What keeps you apart isn't as strong as what binds you. That fact came out at Glenn's trial. Only Myron, Doc Brown, and my husband and I understood everything Adam said when he spoke up for Glenn. Before you do anything, you need to understand it too.'

'The location of the spike?' Hop spat out.

'No. My father adopted me, but his problem was one he shared with Adam. His first wife didn't produce children either and it took his second wife five years to have any children.'

'Are you saying I'm adopted,' Emerson murmured, 'like you?'

'No.' Katie looked past Niles to where Stewart had now given up trying to attract anyone's attention and had bowed his head. 'Stewart Archer never had any trouble siring children, and he helped his friend when there was no other way before the relationship between them soured. You're all set to carry on their feud by killing each other, but you're all brothers. You aren't the Prices and the Archers. You're all Archers.'

Clyde and Niles both stood aghast. Hop flinched, but his shock might have resulted from Katie's failure to mention the location of the spike. Emerson was the first to react. He snorted his breath, his eyes blazing, his face reddening until with a great roar he threw his hand to his gun.

'I'm no Archer!' he shouted, but as his hand reached his gun, Hop reacted and drew his gun. A single shot peeled out, blasting Emerson in the chest. The sheriff staggered back, his half-drawn gun slipping from his fingers as he collapsed to the ground.

Then Hop swung his gun round to aim at Clyde, but as Clyde was just standing there, his bewildered gaze looking at his fallen brother with uncomprehending eyes, he didn't fire. Niles also stood transfixed, leaving Hop to pace to his father's side. He stared down at him as his father creaked his neck up to look at him. Then with a tenderness that belied his previous action, Hop knelt, wrapped his father's blankets more tightly around his chest, and patted his arm.

'I didn't mean,' Stewart croaked, 'for you to do that when I told you to see Myron. I really did just want you to find the spike.'

'And I will,' Hop said as, behind him, Niles walked a pace closer to Clyde, his hand still near to his holster, but when Clyde looked up, he shook his head.

'There's been enough killing here,' he said, 'and I

146

won't kill my . . . my other brother.'

'And neither will I,' Clyde said.

'Leave me out of this,' Hop grunted, leaping to his feet. He swung his gun round to aim it at Clyde, then nodded to the hotel. 'You and I are going to have ourselves a talk.'

Without complaint, Clyde walked towards him, but Niles spoke up.

'Don't do this,' he said.

'Stay out of this, brother,' Hop muttered. 'Our half-brother is about to make amends for everything he's done to our family.'

Hop grabbed Clyde's arm and marched him into the hotel. Only when they'd disappeared from view did Niles hurry to Emerson's side. He rolled him over, then rocked back on his heels at the sight of his lifeless body.

Katie joined him in kneeling down beside Emerson's body, shaking her head until Matlock joined them.

'I'd hoped,' she said, looking up with tears in her eyes, 'that my words might have stopped this happening, not start it.'

'It wasn't your fault,' Matlock said. 'The Prices and the Archers were always like this. I guess it had to end this way.'

'Your husband is right,' Glenn said. 'It could never work for men as loco as Hop and Emerson.' He looked at the hotel. 'But perhaps it can work for Clyde and Niles.'

'It will,' Niles said, 'because I'm about to make it work.'

Niles stood and turned towards the hotel. Glenn stepped to one side to join him.

'You helped me when I was in trouble,' he said. 'I reckon it's time I repaid that help.'

Niles acknowledged him with a nod and both men stood for a moment, to see whether anyone else would offer to help. Matlock stepped forward.

'I may be a politician and of little use in a gunfight.' He glanced around until his eyes lit upon his hired guns. 'But I'd like to end this without more bloodshed. These men will stay here and look after Katie. I will help you talk Hop round.'

With Matlock stepping forward, Glenn looked at Randall, but Randall shook his head.

'You got me all wrong,' he said, backing away a pace and raising his hands. 'I don't rescue nobody when there ain't no bounty involved.'

Glenn reckoned they already had enough help, so he didn't complain. He, Matlock and Niles headed for the hotel's front door. By the door they discussed their tactics and agreed that Niles should head around the back. Then Matlock and Glenn stood on either side of the open doorway. They counted to five then darted inside in one co-ordinated move.

The reception room was deserted.

Side by side they paced to the stairs, Glenn with his gun drawn and Matlock with his hands held at shoulder level in a calming manner. Glenn listened out for anyone moving around inside. He heard nothing. At the bottom of the stairs he gestured for Matlock to try the back room where he'd met Stewart yesterday, while he headed up the stairs.

He was halfway up when he heard talking, low and irritated and coming from the upstairs corridor. He stopped, but at that moment a slap sounded and Clyde staggered into view, his backward-reeling motion implying he'd just been punched. He grabbed hold of the topmost rail to stop himself falling down the stairs. Hop moved into view behind him and punched his jaw, sending him reeling again before he came to a halt, sprawled over the topmost stair with his head arced backwards and lolling.

Hop barely glanced at Glenn as he loomed over Clyde and kicked his chest.

'Stop lying to me,' he roared, 'and tell me where it is.'

Clyde merely returned a gurgling and dazed murmur.

'Hop,' Glenn urged, 'don't harm him.'

'I sure will. We're all after the spike, except he won't admit it.'

'He's done nothing. Your father was wrong. The spike is long gone. But Katie was right and the only secret anyone was worried about keeping was that you and he are brothers. Remember that.'

Glenn had meant his comment to be calming, but Hop's fevered state meant it only went to inflame him even more. He swirled round to face Glenn, then launched himself from the top stair. He caught Glenn around the neck and the two men went tumbling, Glenn's gun clattering to the floor. They rolled, then came to rest standing crouched towards the bottom of the stairs. Glenn wriggled, but Hop had a firm grip of his neck. His eyes were bulging

149

with the effort as he tightened his hands.

Glenn felt his throat close. He grabbed Hop's hands and tried to prise them apart, but they were like iron and he could do nothing but fight for every gasp of air that he could drag into his lungs. Buzzing erupted in his ears and his vision darkened and closed.

In desperation, he tried to drag himself away from Hop's grip, but his assailant followed him. Glenn's back slammed into the stair rail and he leaned back over it, hoping to force Hop to overbalance, but that only helped him to brace himself.

'Wait!' Matlock shouted, emerging from the back room. 'Emerson hired Arnold to find the spike. His actions are questionable enough to mean you might not face charges if you can prove you didn't kill Myron.'

Hop's grip tightened and his eyes flared, suggesting that that was something he could never prove.

'Stay away,' he grunted. 'This is between me and these Prices.'

'But neither of them knows where the golden spike is. I do.'

This time Hop's grip lessened a mite, letting Glenn drag a wheezing breath into his tortured lungs.

'What do you know?' Hop demanded, turning to look down the stairs and dragging Glenn with him.

Matlock gestured to Glenn then to the sprawling Clyde.

'Step away from those people. Then I —'

'You don't make the demands here.' Hop tightened his grip on Glenn's throat and dragged him up close, then drew his gun and thrust it deep into Glenn's stomach. 'Tell me, now!'

'The spike was never for the likes of you,' Matlock said, his tone light and unconcerned. 'Myron knew that, and that's why he never talked and you had to kill him.'

'You do know where it is!' Hop roared. He swung his gun away to aim at Matlock, but long before he'd completed the move, a single shot blasted, the slug tearing into his side. Hop staggered a pace, still clutching hold of Glenn and the two men went rolling down the stairs, entangled. When they'd clattered to the bottom Hop lay still and Glenn easily shrugged out from beneath him.

While fingering his collar, Glenn looked up to see Randall standing in the doorway to the hotel, smoke spiralling from his gun. The two men nodded to each other before Randall turned on his heel and headed away, leaving Matlock to help Glenn to his feet.

They checked that Hop was in fact dead, and while they confirmed that Clyde was only dazed Niles hurried in to join them.

'I'm pleased you're fine,' Niles said, facing Clyde.

'The same can't be said for Hop, or Emerson,' Clyde said. He sighed. 'But they were both hot-headed. I guess it was coming to them one day.'

Niles nodded. 'Then we need to accept that, and you have a new father to get acquainted with.'

The two men looked at each other without malice and although they said nothing more, Glenn reckoned that in their case the bond that linked them would bring them closer. Together, they picked Hop up to take him outside, leaving Matlock and Glenn to follow them, keeping a respectful few paces back.

'So,' Glenn said, glancing at Matlock, 'you do know where the spike is.'

Matlock tapped the side of his nose. 'I'm a politician, not a gunfighter. I just said whatever I needed to say to stop him killing you.'

Matlock stopped to straighten his clothing and bat the dust from his jacket.

'Trouble is,' Glenn said, 'I don't believe you.'

Beyond the door, Katie had edged into their line of sight to check that they were fine. She moved aside to let Clyde and Niles leave. Matlock raised a hand to her and smiled, then swung round on his heel and faced up to Glenn, a harsh glare replacing the warm smile.

'I am a very important man who has stood up for you. Do not repeat a rumour like that again.'

'It's no rumour. It's the truth. You knew that Myron stole it.'

'That is still a rumour.'

'But what is fact is you've bankrolled Adam Price for the last fifteen years.' Glenn stared at Matlock and when he didn't reply, Glenn closed his eyes for a moment, a terrible truth battering at his thoughts. 'You know that Myron stole the spike, but he didn't kill my father. You did. You knew it was in the cabinet, didn't you? You found out from me that the house was empty and while I was out you went there, but Father came back early. That's what happened, isn't it?'

For long moments Matlock didn't reply. Then, with a visible sagging of his shoulders as if conceding that the truth was something he'd wanted to admit for years, he nodded. And when he spoke his voice was low and distant.

'That pretty much describes what happened. Myron Cole hid the spike in the cabinet while he worked out how he could sell it. He came to me because I had contacts, but I got greedy and decided to take it for myself. But I didn't intend to kill him. I really thought he wasn't there. He startled me and I had the spike in my hand. I swung round.' Matlock raised a hand, miming holding the spike then dashed the hand down. 'And I . . . And I . . .'

'And you caved his head in with it?' Glenn watched Matlock give a forlorn nod. 'And what twisted plan made you seek out my sister?'

'But I didn't,' Matlock said, speaking quickly. 'I felt so guilty about what happened to you. I wanted to speak and say that it was an accident, but Adam Price worked out that I did it. He blackmailed me. I went East, but I couldn't escape his grip and so I bankrolled him for long after the money I'd raised had gone. Speaking up for Clyde today was my last duty. But it was never like that with Katie. I love her.'

Glenn sneered. 'Love founded on a lie and a murder.'

'Maybe, but what we have now is real.' Matlock gripped Glenn's arm. 'Are you going to be the one who takes it away from her?'

'Matlock,' Katie called from the door, 'what are you two doing?'

153

Matlock raised his hand and Glenn turned to see Katie peering at them, staring into the darkened reception room.

Without thinking through his actions, Glenn placed a hand on Matlock's shoulder.

'Don't worry,' he said. 'We stopped Hop between us. We're both fine.'

'Then you both must have a great tale to tell.'

'We do,' Matlock said, looking at Glenn, 'don't we? Don't we?'

Glenn didn't want to stay in Black Rock for a moment longer than he needed to, but unfortunately the only stage out of town would come this afternoon and Katie and Matlock would be on it.

Now they were completing their duties in the saloon where, presumably, Matlock was buying everyone a drink and spinning a tale about the events in the hotel, which would secure his reputation and which might even start a legend. Glenn had made an excuse to avoid entering the saloon and joined Clyde and Randall outside the sheriff's office.

'Are you staying?' Clyde said.

'There's nothing for me here,' Glenn said, looking out of town.

'Then maybe I might meet you somewhere else one day.'

'Maybe you will or maybe you won't. But I don't see no reason to.'

'I do.' Clyde swung round to face him. 'None of us may be Prices, but I reckon what links us is more than just blood.'

'Is that your way of apologizing?'

Clyde nodded. 'I guess it is. And if it helps to convince you I know what Emerson did was wrong, I won't be standing for mayor. This town needs an honest man from an honest family. Perhaps my half-brother Niles Archer might do a better job.'

'And perhaps if you realize that, I can accept your apology.'

Clyde acknowledged him with a nod, then left. Glenn noted that he was heading towards the Archer hotel before he turned to Randall.

'Did you get a bounty on Arnold?' he asked.

'Didn't look for one. I shot him for Alan Brown, nothing else.'

'And did you enjoy your revenge?' Glenn asked without thinking, then realized he was talking as much to himself as to Randall.

'Nope. Revenge never brings no joy. It can't bring back the person you wanted to be alive.'

Glenn didn't reply immediately. Randall's comment was helping a thought process to form and perhaps give him an inkling of what he must do.

'And Hop?' he asked. 'Why did you kill him?'

'I only kill for bounty . . . or for friends.'

Glenn couldn't help but smile. 'I said you had more sentiment in you than most bounty hunters.'

'Don't push me, Glenn.' Randall turned, then stopped. 'And what will you do if you're not staying here?'

'Still thinking about it.'

'Well, if you want to try bounty hunting, I reckon you might be good at it. You got the instincts.'

'I didn't think you had partners.'

Randall winced. 'Not a partner. Now that Arnold's dead, I'd welcome having a worthwhile rival.'

CHAPTER 14

The stage was almost ready to move out.

Glenn had said his goodbyes to Katie, and had duly ignored Matlock. He had no doubt that Matlock loved her, and no doubt that he ought to tell Katie the truth, but destroying the life she'd built for herself felt just as bad as not saying anything.

And Randall was right – revenge at this late stage would bring nobody any joy.

Randall had left town some hours ago. With Glenn making his peace with Clyde Price, and perhaps gaining another friend in Niles Archer, he could stay in town and make a life for himself here. But perhaps not everyone here would trust him after everything that had happened, and so he had to move on.

He loitered outside the Archer hotel, watching the driver check that the baggage on the roof was secure. Presently, Katie leaned from the window to wave goodbye. He knew that now he had to say what he'd learned or never say it. He pushed himself from the wall and walked to the stage. He held her hand through the window, smiling, but then, in a sudden decision, he opened the door and swung himself inside to sit beside her, and opposite to Matlock.

Aside from Matlock's hired guns, they were the only people inside.

'Are you. . . ?' she asked. 'Are you coming with us?'

'I guess there's nothing for me here and I don't fancy following Randall.' He shrugged. 'Perhaps East might be the direction to go for me too. You certainly made it work for you.'

Glenn looked at Matlock, who returned his gaze with his lips pursed, clearly avoiding breathing while he waited to see what he'd say.

'That's marvellous,' Katie said, clasping his hand, oblivious to the tension between the two men. 'I'm sure you'll love it there.'

'I will.' Glenn fixed his gaze on Matlock. 'In fact, your husband was kind enough to offer me a job. And I reckon I'll take him up on his generous offer.'

Matlock's eyes flared and he let out an explosion of air.

'I did what?' he blustered. 'I can't—'

Katie bounded out of her seat and her huge hug cut off the rest of his comment before he could utter it. Her movement let Glenn see that the driver was looking in on them to check that Glenn really did want to leave with the stage. Glenn nodded, then edged to the side to look at Matlock over his sister's shoulder.

'What do you think?' Glenn asked, his tone neutral.

'I suppose that is possible,' Matlock muttered. He extricated himself from Katie's arms and spoke

quickly and commandingly. 'But you have to understand that a man in my position offering a job to a
man who was convicted of murder can cause problems.'

'I know, and that was why it was so generous and
brave of you to offer me such a *senior* and well-paid
position in your office.'

'Senior?' Matlock murmured. 'Is that entirely
appropriate for a man who was so unappreciative of
Adam's actions?'

Katie furrowed her brow, clearly confused as to
what Matlock had meant, but Glenn caught the infer-
ence that he was accepting a bribe to keep quiet
about what he knew. Such an action had been
furthest from Glenn's thoughts and so the slight
didn't concern him.

'The seniority doesn't appeal to me,' he said, 'and
neither does the money. I'm just pleased that you
and I will be able to spend plenty of time together.
We can get to understand each other and check that
we both have Katie's interests at heart.'

'Yes,' Matlock murmured through gritted teeth. 'I
suppose we can do that.'

'And I can check every day that my sister has made
a wise choice for her husband.'

'But I did,' Katie said in an unconcerned manner.
Her pleasant comment stopped Glenn from offering
any more veiled threats.

But Matlock's flared eyes showed he understood
Glenn's meaning. Glenn had accepted his father's
death was an accident only because of Katie, but if he
ever had reason to suppose Matlock wasn't putting

159

her interests first. . . .

With much hollering the stage lurched to a start. Glenn settled back on his seat to look out of the window. He watched Black Rock slip away and waited for a new land and new possibilities to open up ahead.

But he knew one thing for sure: no matter what the future held for him, he would never return to Black Rock.